ECHOES OF THE DIVINE

Other titles by
Danielle Ackley-McPhail

The Eternal Cycle Series
Yesterday's Dreams
Tomorrow's Memories
Today's Promise

The Eternal Wanderings Series
Eternal Wanderings

The Bad-Ass Faerie Tale Series
The Halfling's Court
The Redcap's Queen
The High King's Fool
(forthcoming)

Baba Ali and the Clockwork Djinn
(with Day Al-Mohamed)

Daire's Devils

The Literary Handyman
Build-A-Book Workshop
More Tips From the Handyman

The Ginger KICK! Cookbook

Short Fiction
A Legacy of Stars
Transcendence
Consigned to the Sea
Flash in the Can
The Kindly One
Dawns a New Day
The Die Is Cast
(with Mike McPhail)

ECHOES OF THE DIVINE

DANIELLE ACKLEY-McPHAIL

Pennsville, NJ

PUBLISHED BY
Paper Phoenix Press
A division of eSpec Books
PO Box 242
Pennsville, NJ 08070
www.especbooks.com

ISBN: 978-1-956463-59-0
ISBN (ebook): 978-1-956463-58-3

"Looking Back" originally published in *Athena's Daughters*, Silence in the Library Press.
"To Reach for Distant Shores" originally published in *Mermaids 13*, Padwolf Publishing.
"Windows to the Soul" originally published in *After Punk*, eSpec Books.
"On the Wings of an Angel" originally published in *In an Iron Cage*, Dark Quest Books.
"Trouble on the Water" originally published in *Trouble on the Water*, Dark Quest Books.
"Angel de la Muerte" originally published in *A Cast of Crows*, NeoParadoxa.
"Ala al-Din and the Cave of Wonders" originally published in *Grimm Machinations,* eSpec Books.

Interior Design: Danielle McPhail
Cover Art: www.shutterstock.com
Steampunk vintage poster, bridge banner background with cogs and gears on canvas paper © Magergram
Fortune Teller Hand with Palmistry diagram, hand-drawn all seeing eye © Smiling Fox
Sprockets © Dn Br

Cover Design: Mike and Danielle McPhail, McP Digital Graphics
Copyediting: Greg Schauer

Dedication

To David Lee Summers,
the most dashing and authentic steampunk I know,
as well as one hell of a great friend.

Acknowledgments

My deepest thanks to Mano Divina and the Divine Hand Ensemble for graciously giving me permission to include their names and likeness in the story "Echoes of the Divine," for which their performance was the inspiration. Though the story did not turn out as I had envisioned, I am happy to have finally written it... *ten years* after first getting the idea. Never give up on inspiration, creativity comes in its own time.

Thanks are also due to Ef Deal and Dale Russell for beta-reading that story for me on such short notice, as well as for all of their encouragement and support on everything I do.

Contents

Looking Back

"Lady Clara! Lady Clara!" a voice called out.

The Right Honorable Claramina Evangelista Pemberton, Countess Chadsworth—the very image of propriety in her dainty hat, rose velvet walking gown, white gloves, and pearl-buttoned boots—stopped very still, took a deep, imperious breath that was warning in itself, and slowly pivoted on one heel. Her already alabaster skin paled further until it bore the aspect of shaved ice as her brown eyes darkened to the hard luster of anthracite. The gentry swarmed the park this afternoon, impeccable in their finery, quite eager to see and be seen. All around her she heard their murmurs and gasps, and not a few sly titters from those glad to witness her touched by even this slight scandal. The rumor-mongers were in bliss. Though she careful schooled her expression to display nothing of the sort, within she was mortified.

Seemingly unaware, Fritz Langstrom, wearing a leather duster marred by oil and dirt and scorch marks, hurried toward her, a battered set of goggles perched atop his head. The man was coarse... American... brilliant. And, it would seem, completely ignorant of the conventions of polite society. Stepping quite above his station, he reached out, ready to clasp her arm in a most unseemly manner. Beside her, Lionel, Lord Barrington, a distant cousin and her escort of the afternoon, drew a sharp breath and stepped forward, deflecting the commoner's touch.

Langstrom barely blinked as he went on. "Lady Clara, wait 'til you see... I dare say... we have success!" His words came out in something of a pant, hurried, urgent, but certain enough to cool her anger. In the barest of touches, Clara laid her gloved fingertips on Lionel's sleeve but kept her attention full upon the inventor's words. "You instructed me to inform you immediately…"

"Cousin," Clara said to her companion, cutting off the interloper before he could say too much. "Might I impose upon you to summon the carriage?"

The gentleman stared at her with shock and affront clearly visible in his gaze, if not his expression, but he did not argue and went to do as she bade. Clara allowed him a slight, encouraging smile before he looked away. That smile quite disappeared as she turned to the inventor upon whom she bestowed her patronage. "You," she said in quiet, clipped tones that carried no further than from her lips to Langstrom's ears, "will return yourself to your laboratory by whatever means took you from it, and you will never again accost me so, am I understood?"

"But you will come?"

"I shall, and may God or the Devil help you if your achievement does not out-strip your offense, for no mere man will be able to. Now go!" The man hurried away as she instructed, clearly content to know that she would follow, and obviously overeager to return to whatever breakthrough had inspired such unacceptable behavior. Drawing her proud demeanor firmly about her, Clara remained straight and proper where she stood and waited for her escort to return. Deep within, however, excitement akin to that which Langstrom openly displayed coursed through her noble veins. Outwardly, a spark of satisfaction glittering in her eyes betrayed the only sign she felt anything at all.

It took no small effort to convince Lord Barrington to cut short their afternoon's engagement, but Clara managed. Even as his carriage rattled away down the lane, she hurriedly descended the front stairs she had just climbed and made her way around the manor toward the path leading to the carriage house. Once clear from sight, she lifted the front hem of her gown several inches and lengthened her stride.

If Father were alive to see her he would have been scandalized.

Her teeth ground in a very unladylike manner at the thought. If *dear* Father had any care for her wellbeing, she would not be forced to consort with inventors *or* Americans, let alone both in one base-born specimen. With the senseless hunting death of Lord Chadsworth, Clara found herself quite alone, left with a modest endowment and the burden of managing the ancestral home now belonging to her father's heir — her cousin, Rockford — until he should surface. It had been several years already and the last of the special investigators she'd engaged had given up the search as hopeless. She found herself torn, unsure if she should be glad rather than distressed. Not that she did not have fond memories of Rockford from her youth. At one time she had entertained dreams of courtship and betrothal, but that was long ago. She now had doubts concerning her own fate once he returned to assume his title, for surely he had long since taken a wife. Such a one would not care for a rival in her domain, particularly one who had at one point had the governing of the household. And yet Clara's heart held a fading hope that she was wrong; that Rockford was not attached and that there might yet be more between them. And so she had become a patroness of the sciences. She had, in fact, invested her own endowment provisioning Fritz Langstrom's laboratory. She had exhausted all conventional means of tracking Rockford; now they looked to the sciences to gain any possible hint of his whereabouts.

As she drew close to the carriage house, it was impossible to tell if Langstrom was even inside, given that the windows were shuttered and draped in such a manner that there was no means of seeing through the glass. Anxious, she lengthened her strides further until she near ran in a shameful fashion. Stopping a moment as she gained the door, she allowed her breath and color to settle before she entered. The air carried the faint scent of her late mother's roses from the nearby garden. The perfume served as an anchor. Each breath she drew restored and reinforced the demeanor of *Lady* Pemberton.

As if acting with the utmost propriety could ever countermand the scandal if my arrangement with Langstrom were discovered... She pushed the uncomfortable thought aside and carefully unpinned her hat from her upswept, sable hair, leaving it and her white gloves beside the door, where they would not be ruined. She then gripped the doorknob and gave a sharp twist, moving across the threshold with purpose. Only by will alone did she manage not to flinch back from the brilliance of the thermolampes ringing the single room within. When she'd had a caretaker, this space had served as that one's room of all purpose: cooking, eating, sleeping, and fortnightly, bathing. In her desperation, Lady Clara had gambled. Letting the caretaker go, she installed in his place her inventor and set him the task of discovering the means by which to find Rockford.

Stepping from the entryway, she grabbed her full-length, stained leather duster—cousin to the one Langstrom wore—from its customary hook by the door. As she slipped it on over her dress and secured it, making sure the coat fully covered the finer fabric, she moved across the room to the massive worktable that now dominated the space. Not once did she glance away from Fritz Langstrom or the contraption before which he stood, and yet she managed to navigate her way past massive coils of copper wire and bundles of brass, copper, and glass tubes, sacks full of coal and iron gears, and barrels of dark, rank oil which lubricated the inner workings of the device.

The inventor gave a start at her voice, all but for his hands, which remain absolutely steady as they made adjustments to the plethora of connectors. "You're here!"

She presumed he beamed at her, as was his usual habit, but it was difficult to tell as the goggles that had been perched atop his head were now drawn down, a small, magnifying lens swung into place over his right eye. Clara pursed her lips disapprovingly. Langstrom was like an ill-disciplined hound, yapping and clambering and *familiar*, without restraint. She was not at all comfortable with that aspect of their interaction. Carefully, he set the delicate watchmaker's tools with which he currently worked upon the table and hurried to her side, pushing the goggles up until they again perched atop his head.

A subtle change in his demeanor unsettled her further. Her back went rigid and her chin lifted. "Well?" she said as she arched a delicate brow toward the device he had been working on.

"Yes… of course," he said, his eyes widening ever so slightly. "I have not yet tested it, per your instructions, but it is ready, and now that you are present… Please, if you will join me over here, by the Futuraositor." A muscle in her cheek twitched faintly as he uttered that infernal name with which he had christened her machine. She spoke not a word, her eyes alone revealed her displeasure. Instead she watched as he ran a lightly oiled rag over the invention, wiping away any dirt or dust that might interfere with the process. It took more than a few minutes as his so-called Futuraositor took up three quarters of the rather large worktable. Clara waited impatiently, tapping the toe of her pearl-buttoned boot against the worn boards of the floor. She watched as he adjusted dials, opening some valves, while closing others, and precisely positioned various levers. When all was set, he used an ironmonger's gauntlet to slide a brazier filled with lit coals into the belly of the beast, beneath where she knew a rather costly copper boiler had recently been installed. Within moments she heard the hiss of steam and tasted hot iron with each breath. Water began to boil in an array of hollow, glass tubes mapping the surface of the… *Futuraositor*… like veins. Those delicate tubes continued across a few inches of empty air to connect with a narrow brass box framing two sheets of the most perfect glass she had ever seen. Her breath caught in a gasp as the space between those sheets slowly filled with a swirling fog that behaved rather different than the steam she'd expected.

This was new. "What…?" she managed.

Langstrom anticipated her query: "Aether," he said, his response distracted as he reached over and adjusted the settings on an object that looked like an ornate astrolabe centrally placed atop the mechanism.

"This," he said in hushed, reverent tones, "is what has brought us to this moment. This is the guarantor of our success…"

Clara found it maddening the way he went on. "And *this* is…?"

Langstrom's gaze snapped to her as if he only now truly realized she were there. His eyes had obvious trouble remaining focused upon her, straying to his grand invention, before gravitating back. "This, my Lady Clara, is the diurnalscope." His voice became animated rather than distracted as he caressed the orb and explained this latest innovation: a device to track and orient the Futuraositor to the motion of the celestial bodies circling the Earth, past, present, and future. "Astrology is the key," he said. "By mapping the diurnal arc of the stars, it should be completely possible to glimpse any place you seek, and in any point in time."

"But how can it possibly work?" Clara did not try to keep her skepticism from her voice. Langstrom did not seem to notice.

"It is simple! Everything around us is made up of aether… it is the fundamental component of reality." The fervor in his expression unnerved her. "By calculating the diurnal arc of the stars, in this case forward, and projecting those calculations through the aether lens," he pointed to the glass box and its swirling contents, "we align now with then and can glimpse whatever is in a given space for the point in time which we desire. Simple!"

The look he cast upon her was eager and hopeful and proud all at once, as if more than pleasing her, he sought to make her proud. Unfortunate for him, a full third, if not more, of what Langstrom said made absolutely no sense to her. That did not matter, though, as she held tight to his claims: They would focus their attempts upon the future in the hopes of discovering the key to locating Rockford.

(She refused to consider they might learn of more dire things.)

Her chest rose and fell more rapidly with each breath as she watched Langstrom attach a bowl-shaped assemblage of riveted brass plates to the back, upright facing of his device. It pointed toward the sole section of table untouched by clutter or machine, the space right beyond the window-like glass.

Langstrom turned one final knob, then snatched a second set of goggles from the table surface and hurried toward her. Swiftly drawing them down over her eyes, he then lightly, but firmly gripped her by the elbow and drew her away behind a thick, woven-metal screen before she could protest either action.

She tugged her arm away and rounded on the man. Her cheeks burned uncomfortably, as did her arm where his fingers had held her, but before she could voice her protest the machine's hissing became a whine, and then a sharp-pitched whistle, and the air became heavy upon her, pressing against her ears, forcing the breath from her chest more thoroughly than any whalebone corset had yet managed. Clara gasped and looked toward the machine, just visible through the small gaps in the woven screen. The device appeared infernal indeed, with the glow of red-hot coals reflecting from the tempered glass tubes and steam billowing throughout the cottage until it would not have surprised her to have the Great Deceiver step forth from its depths. Unconsciously, she clutched at Fritz Langstrom's arm and did not even take exception when he patted her hand reassuringly.

"Watch," he said in a voice as reverent as any fanatic.

Clara complied without question as the red glow gave way to blazing white heat and the cry of the pressurized steam threatened to pierce her eardrum. The machine… the table… the very cottage walls began to shake. She swayed as she felt her heartbeat in every inch of her body; her vision blurred and her breath came so labored she scarcely noticed the taste of coal dust on the moist, heavy air. As the thermolampes flared, then flickered, and the room took on a darker aspect, Clara grew concerned she was about to have the vapors as she never had before.

The moment passed, but Clara's pulse and breathing didn't slow until the clouds of steam faded to a light mist, then to nothing. Langstrom scrambled past the protective screen, grabbing her hand to draw her after him. She barely noticed. Her body shook and she told herself she merely shivered, the condition brought on by the sudden film of chilled, dew-like moisture coating every surface in the cottage, including herself. She refused to acknowledge the dread-steeped excitement pricking every inch of her skin.

Eagerness and caution were at war within her.

Langstrom, and thus Clara, stopped beside the main housing of his invention. She looked up where his attention was transfixed: upon the brass dish she'd watched him attach earlier — was it truly just moments ago? What she had not noted then were the coiled wires at the center of that riveted, highly polished surface, nestled in the depression, now pointing like a finger of white-gold light through the glass-encased aether. She found it difficult to tell through the swirling mist, but the light seemed to touch upon some shape on the far side.

"Astounding!" the inventor muttered. Again he grabbed her arm — she had never in her life been so thoroughly manhandled as she had this day — and yet she could not resist his tugging or the excitement that echoed her own state.

More accurate to say, she had no desire to.

Together they crept around the visual barrier. Clara felt her eyes go nearly as wide as the brass dish. There... on the previously empty table surface... was a... *thing*. A rather large wooden object shaped somewhat like an overly wide clock, with a rounded top and five small knobs on the front. Where the clock face would be there was inset a slightly curved pane of thick, smoky glass about the size of the palm of her hand, the likes of which she had never set eyes upon. An etched brass plate secured to the front declared it a "Televisor."

She found the whole of it quite perplexing.

Clara's head shook slowly from side to side. This thing did not quite seem what she'd been promised, in any manner that she could tell, though surely she could not dispute Langstrom had succeeded in something.

She would have dared reach out to touch the cabinet, were she not suddenly grabbed about the waist and hefted into the air. The inventor swung her as if she were a child sharing a bit of glee. Lady Claramina Evangelista Pemberton brought her hands smacking sharply down upon the man's arms and pushed herself free, nearly falling in the process.

"Never! Touch me again!" she snapped as she scrambled to regain her balance.

He just stood there, his expression stunned and his chest heaving. Something different burned in his gaze that overshadowed even his earlier fervor in intensity. That look pinned her in place and doused her anger in a way she could not explain. She glanced hastily away, heaved out a sigh, and smoothed her hand over her hair and down her person, trying to restore some sense of decorum before meeting the man's eyes as directly as she could manage given the way he unsettled her so.

"What," she asked abruptly, "is that, and what does it do?" It looked like a refined version of one of Langstrom's own inventions so she presumed he would have some answer.

Langstrom tilted his head ever so slightly to the side in a considering manner, looking from her, to the object, and back again. "I don't… know… *yet!*"

Clara shivered and with haste took herself away to the safety of the manor house, leaving the inventor to his tinkering.

After that first occasion, she judiciously decided that her presence was no longer required during the activation of the machine. The memory of the first event was enough as it was to give her a case of the nerves; repeat occurrences would have quite unbalanced her constitution. Not that waiting in the manor was any better for her disposition, but most assuredly it was safer.

As much as she told herself that, her thoughts often wandered on their own toward the carriage house.

Twice Langstrom summoned her. Twice he presented her with confounding objects both wondrous and strange. Langstrom had yet to construe the true nature of the three presumably future-fetched artifacts, though seemingly not for lack of effort… or expense. His attempts were hindered — or so he claimed — by the fact that shortly after their appearance, said objects disappeared, quite fading away. Clara had yet to witness this phenomenon herself.

Her patience was nearly exhausted and she had to wonder — even though she herself was in attendance when first the Futuraositor had supposedly drawn an object from the aether — was Langstrom deceiving her? Much of what he presented to her bore some passing similarity to his own, less refined workings… though it remained that she could not explain the sudden appearance of that first wonder in a space where she knew it had not been previously. Still... it was possible the man was by some means merely presenting his own inventions as fetched items. These doubts, in combination with her worries for Rockford, had her quite in a state, for — as far as she could determine — they were no closer to spying his whereabouts than before.

The third time the summons came Clara could fairly hear the excitement in the inventor's voice even over the wire of the distance speaker of his own contriving. Lowering the still vibrating air bladder from her ear and resting it back in its cup, she hurried to the cottage.

Langstrom met her at the door. His gaze held a glee that had grown steadily each time the Futuraositor "retrieved" an item. Excitement sparked through him like he was some organic Jacob's Ladder. (There was a faint protest at the back of Clara's mind that she even knew the name, or enough of what it was to make such a comparison. Proper ladies did not know such things. Of course, as time passed, being a proper lady seemed to hold much less appeal.) She trembled with the mingled trepidation and anticipation coursing through her own veins.

"Come! Come!" Langstrom called to her. He took a few scuttling steps toward his device, then half turned and edged back toward her, his arms beckoning enthusiastically. It was like a disturbing dance.

Clara ignored him. Taking her time, she donned her customary duster, safeguarding her garments with utmost care, and only then moved with controlled decorum across the room, Langstrom bobbing before her like an anxious vanguard. The journey was not as simple as in past visits; the carriage house had gathered all manner of indecipherable things. She nudged them aside with the barest of touches as she wove through the clutter toward the machination. She pursed her lips skeptically as she glanced at the space beyond the aether lens, to which Langstrom gestured with a flourish.

On the scarred worktable lay a broadsheet, but one printed in a manner she had never before seen. The bulk of it was thick. Many, many pages of clear, crisp type, but upon a thin paper of the coarsest kind. She saw no sign of excess ink transfer or smudging, and yet, though the materials were clearly inferior, the techniques astounded her. On the very paper was an image of a man appearing almost as he would if he were standing before her. This was no daguerreotype or etching done by an artist. There was even color on the page, though oddly faded. The page was dated Saturday, April 25, 1970. Clara looked from the paper to Langstrom and drew a shuddering breath. There was no manner by which Langstrom could have produced such a thing himself.

A giggle escaped her as she realized she at last beheld incontrovertible proof that the Futuraositor worked. It had not been comfortable to doubt him. Her hand flew to her mouth to smother the sound, but to no effect. She continued to laugh until Langstrom joined her, his full-bodied bass rumbling through the magpie's nest the room had become. The laughter did not stop until she went into a fit of coughing as gas and coal dust clogged her throat unchecked. Langstrom served her several sharp blows to the back before she waved him off. And even then she could not restrain the uncharacteristic smile upon her lips as she leaned forward over the pages.

The smile quickly faded.

"This is gibberish." She turned accusing eyes upon the inventor. "What is a "jetliner"? And a "movie star?" What good was a broadsheet from the future if it made no sense to her? Still, it was closer to achieving her goal than anything else they had yet retrieved. With time, she was confident of her success in discerning their meaning, perhaps finding something to guide her, though she could not imagine what. She refolded the pages and tucked them beneath her left arm then turned to Langstrom.

"Work the machine again," she ordered.

Langstrom looked doubtfully from her to the Futuraositor.

"We dare not so soon, my lady." His tone was cautious. "The boiler must cool down or the building pressure could cause an explosion."

Once before, early on in their efforts, she had been witness to just such a mishap (and thus the procurement of the woven metal screen). On that occasion, the housing of the machine, the very metal itself, had glowed as red as the coals that powered it, while steam as dark as smoke billowed from the riveted seams. The stench of hot metal had nigh choked her such that the mere memory inspired a tickle in her throat.

She suppressed the pending cough.

The current incarnation of the device bore little resemblance to its ill-fated predecessor. Clearly Langstrom was being overcautious. And was she not the patroness here? Clara placed the tip of her finger to her lips and spat upon it, then reached out her right hand and in the barest of touches ran it across the exterior of the machine. Her wetted skin sizzled and reddened, but no blister formed. With every ounce of entitlement in her blue-blooded veins—powered by every speck of desperation hidden in her heart — she drew herself up as she turned back to the inventor. Her head cocked, and then her brow rose, while her chin lifted.

"Work. The machine. Again," she enunciated precisely, "Or leave here this instant and I will work it myself."

A change overcame Langstrom's eyes, as if something within him had at long last awoke. For the first time that she could remember, all good cheer fled his demeanor. He clenched his jaw in clear frustration; his eyes narrowing ever so slightly, as his face went from a white paler than her own to deepest red and back again. He showed uncharacteristic restraint. "And miss all the excitement? Not hardly." His tone was forced.

Langstrom shooed her away toward the protective, woven screen, thrusting a pair of goggles into her hands as he did so. She accepted them with much the same grace with which they were given. Settling them with care over her eyes she turned and glided through the clutter to her place, there to wait impatiently as Langstrom went about his preparations with considerably less alacrity than in his past efforts.

In the shadow of the screen she watched intently. Soon. Very soon, she was certain of it.

The smile returned.

This working of the machine was different. Where before the cottage merely trembled in reaction, it now shook as if the earth quaked beneath it, as if, like ancient Jericho itself, the walls would come down. The steam filling the cottage was dark and caustic, and the crackle in the air hurt her ears. Despite the goggles and the screen, Clara squeezed her eyes tight and hunched away, unashamedly hiding herself in the shadow of the American. The air burned around her with the heat and a high-pitched keen came from the direction of the Futuraositor. Beneath his breath, she heard Langstrom swear and felt him tense all over. He did not move toward the machine though. In fact, he hunched himself much in the same manner she did.

The very foundation of the earth moved beneath them.

Suddenly there sounded a loud pop, followed by a roar. Stings pelted the bare skin of her cheeks and hands. Some force punched hard against her shoulder with the might of a kicking mule. Clara screamed. Langstrom pivoted toward her, his body curving protectively over her crouched form. Her eyes flew open and she stared in open-mouthed horror from beneath the shadow of his arm. Molten glass seemed to fill the air, as did flames, and bits of metal pinged off of every surface. Smoke, blue-tinged and swirling oddly, mingled with the newly unleashed aether, not yet burned up or dispersed. From the midst of the destruction staggered the silhouette of a man. Clara gasped and clutched at Langstrom, recalling the last time she'd sheltered behind this screen and her then-fanciful musings about what forces might come forth from the shrouding steam of their invention…

Terror gripped her. Did she imagine the odor of sulfur pinched her nostrils? Or was her earlier imagining now revealed prophetic? What manner of evil came forth from the infernal machine? And then the man-shape cleared the smoke and flame; Clara saw his countenance and swayed as she lost consciousness.

The Devil wore Rockford's face.

Coolness bathed her cheeks, a rough, moist cloth followed by the faintest kiss of a breeze. Clara frowned and drew a breath that quavered faintly as it again left her. Again the cloth bathed her skin and she had the impulse to frown, though not the wherewithal to follow through. Though she willed it, she could not seem to open her eyes. She would have drawn herself away, but lacked the strength. Instead she made a weak attempt to wave the interloper off.

The scream the effort wrenched from her echoed through the room. Reflexively she drew her right arm close to her, only to cry out again as any attempt at movement woke agony in her shoulder.

"Careful, careful… ducks."

A man's voice assaulted her ears. His manner of speech was British. Though spoken softly, it was oddly harsh, brash even, making the American seem almost polished and dignified in comparison.

"You've done yourself a right treat, here," the strange voice went on. "You keep flailing about and you'll undo my bandaging." That was when her mind took note that there were slight tones of Liverpool in those words, only more entrenched than ever she had heard from the stable lad she employed.

Lady Claramina Evangelista Pemberton found the strength to open her eyes.

They nearly closed again as the room swirled uncomfortably around her, like the aether that had been trapped between the once-perfect glass. But for the burning pain at her right shoulder she would have given in to the vapors once more. And then she looked up and fought to focus on the blurred form beside where she lay.

She shuddered.

Standing over her was the one she had mistaken for both Rockford and the Devil in one. She dare believe even now she'd had reason for both, though the resemblance to her cousin was only slight. This one had hair black as pitch and eyes the color of warm brandy. The strong lines of his face were marred by dreadful cuts that did not look out of place upon the rogue. He looked altogether more dangerous than her cousin, who was something of a dandy, though the stranger's odd clothing spoke to his having an air of the peacock as well, when not singed about the edges.

A part of her searched for some glimmer of herself in that face, but there was none.

Clara drew bravado around her like a shield.

"I will have you whipped for touching my person."

The stranger had the impertinence to grin at her. "Thanks, and all, but I'm not into that scene."

Clara stared at him, perplexed, trying to decipher his words. He made less sense to her than Langstrom did. In fact, he was as unfathomable as the broadsheet that had brought them to this pass. Feeling somewhat frantic in ever-increasing measure, she darted looks about her, seeking some manner of deliverance. They remained in the cottage, in a shadowy alcove off to the side. The window had been opened, but afforded little light as dusk settled outside.

Inside the smoke had dissipated and one or two thermolampes still burned. For the most part the interior of the cottage seemed to bear only superficial scars from the recent explosion. The flames clearly had not been as bad as they had seemed; a blackened wool blanket covered the broken carcass of the Futuraositor. The air was still heavy with an acrid stench, a mingling of burnt oil, aether, and scorched wool. Beneath her, she idly noted, was nothing but coarse sheets over a straw-tick mattress. Presumably this was the inventor's bed upon which she lay.

That was when her thoughts caught up with the current situation. "Where is Langstrom? What have you done with him?"

"What?" The man's brow dipped. "Oh, him. Out cold, a few scratches, knot on the back of his head… I made him comfortable beneath the table. Was the only place there was room."

The relief she felt was somewhat deeper than she would have anticipated. She strained to see past the stranger, concerned tightening her features. Foolish of her, really, to take her eyes off the stranger; he reached out for her again.

Gasping, she tried to scramble back, to push upright to better defend herself. Dizziness overcame her. A quiet groan crept from between her lips.

"Oh, give over! I'm just cleaning off the blood!"

Clara tried to puzzle once more the meaning of the stranger's outburst but with no success. She darted out her left hand and plucked the rag from his grip, dabbing it ineffectually at her brow where something thick and viscous left her skin tight.

The young man bestowed upon her such a look of incredulity Clara almost felt compelled to laugh. She restrained the impulse, suspecting the sound would come out somewhat crazed. Then his eyes narrowed ever so slightly and his chin raised the slightest degree. Saying nothing, he took a step back from the bedstead. But for the hair, in this light he so looked like her cousin, only Rockford's hair was the caramel color of a strong, dark tea.

"Your name, sir?"

A low moan from across the room forestalled his answer. Her eyes closed briefly in relief at the sound, to hear for herself that Langstrom's fate had not been worse. She groaned at her folly that had caused all of this.

The stranger pivoted and went to check on Langstrom. As he did so, Clara used the moment to take stock of her person. The duster had been removed, as had the torn sleeve of her day dress. Her shoulder had been bandaged but her arm remained shockingly bare. Faint traces of crimson showed through the reasonably clean rag binding her wound. It took her but a moment to realize the cloth bore familiar lace eyelets along the overlapping edges. She gasped with shock and drew her legs beneath her, under the skirt of her gown, and propped herself up against the simple headboard.

"What, you expected me to use something lying around here, maybe?" The stranger's eyes swept from one greasy, grimy surface to another throughout the cottage. "Hmmm... bad idea, you think?"

Her lips tightened in response but she did not engage him in verbal battle. "Is all well with Langstrom?"

"He'll live, but once he wakes, he'll have the mother of all headaches."

"Then I ask again, sir, your name?"

Instead of answering, the man wandered the cottage his head shaking from side to side, his hand trailing over Langstrom's bits and pieces. Her hand clutched the blood-smudged cloth she'd taken from him as he crouched of a sudden and came to his feet with the relatively unscathed broadsheet in his hands.

The stranger turned to look at her, his gaze reproving. "What are you playing at, ducks?"

Giving back a bit of what he'd given, she raised her chin and pressed her lips closed tight.

He scowled and drew close, the paper clutched in his fist. "I don't know how you've managed it," he said, huffing out a breath as he gestured around him, "but you had no right to yank me here, unrooting me from my own time."

Clara sputtered, and then drew herself up stiff and proper, the picture of affronted nobility. "I have no idea what you mean..."

"Oh! Give over! I'm not touched in the head. I'm here, you're here... it's my home, but in a state it's not been in for near one hundred years.

"It's the same place. I've seen photos enough of what it'd been to know where I am. I've seen pictures of you... or one anyway, enough I recognize you, *Clara*." He leaned closer, tossing the paper in her lap. "Interesting as it is to meet you face to face, you got to quit mucking about before you do serious harm!"

Clara gasped and swallowed convulsively as the reality of his words penetrated her shock. They'd done it! Not only had the machine worked, but here was one who if she understood correctly could perhaps tell her what she most wanted to know, but dare not ask. Could he know of her future... of Rockford's? She leaned toward him, the paper rustled in her lap as hope crept into her features, warming her cheeks. Her breath came a little faster.

"You know me?"

"Not the point... you're messing with dangerous stuff here. You can't look at something without changing it. That means no peeking!"

She scrambled forward then, swallowing a whimper as she moved too fast for her injured arm. There was no rustle of paper. Clara barely noticed that the substantial weight of the broadsheet was gone from across her legs. "Tell me..."

He looked at her as if she were the one fit for the asylum. "Will you listen to what I'm saying, woman! I like my life just as it is. Leave off on the future before you screw it up!"

"But…"

"*Gah*, I never imagined you for a spoilt brat. I don't know what you hope to get at with all this, but I can't figure it's anything better than what you'll toss off by messing with what you shouldn't. Why steal peeks at the future when you should be building it?"

Though most of his words might confound her, the sense of what he said rang harsh in her ears. She felt no better than a silly child. Clara drew in a sharp breath as he backed away toward the carcass of the machine. Toward Langstrom. Her eyes widened as the man stepped into a pool of light. Cracks riddled his form; fine cracks, grown subtly wider as she stared in horrified fascination. From the fissures, swirls of aether rose to wreath about him. She trembled as she realized his edges had gone quite transparent. He stopped moving as he came beside the shrouded machine.

"What have you squandered on this, Clara? What have you already let slip away to get whatever you're after?" With a tug from his ethereal hand he bared the wreckage of her endeavor. The remains of her personal fortune… her dreams. And worse, she found, the battered body of her American. From beneath the worktable, Fritz glanced over at her, his intentions as clear in his gaze as they had always been, had she not been willfully blind to them.

She blinked furiously against threatening tears.

"Tomorrow comes soon enough, Clara. Don't be in such a hurry to get there."

Clara felt herself nodding, shame burning hot across her cheeks.

"Your name, sir," she asked again, all arrogance gone from the near whisper.

He smiled, and she knew the answer even before he spoke. "It's Rockford."

As this other Rockford faded like the very aether he'd come from, Clara's eyes remained locked with Fritz's. There was a question there she wasn't quite ready to answer, but she could allow that the future she'd once envisioned would never be the same.

To Reach for Distant Shores

A Tale from the World of the Silver Moon

The answers to my dreams were brought to me by a flash storm come up from the south off the sea — violent, sudden, unexpected. The winds rarely drove from that direction, but when they did it was gloriously primal. I could feel them in the fine bones of my body, like the warning my whisker hairs sent when something dangerous loomed close by.

While my sisters and brothers dove down deep at the threat of the storm, I wended my way upward, to peer from the lee of the rocks jutting from the slapping waves, my eyes trained on the water's surface and the skies, avidly watching for the signs that would come swift and sudden and much too late for any about on the surface to heed. In the distance, barely heard, the air rumbled warning of the tempest's approach. With vague interest I noticed narrow, oblong bladders high up in the sky, floating like the jellies beneath the waves, right down to the tendrils dangling from their core. Tiny trailers of electric static crackled like an eel's warning across the bladder's skin before the energy was gone, dispersed on the quickening wind.

Again my bones shivered as the storm drew ever closer. This was the moment when down close to the water the air fell too still. My eyes scanned the sea, drawn by vibrations on the surface. To my left a large mass drifted by like a rare leviathan risen from the depths in the dark hour to let the light of the unseen moon brush its skin. It was a made thing, a ship, filled with man-things scurrying about at this first hint of the coming storm. As the vessel passed, thunder rumbled faintly in the distance, popping closer and closer. The rapidly darkening clouds lit up and sudden trails of lightning danced down from the sky, colliding with each other and the mass on the water, high up where thin, straight branches rose like webbed fingers to touch the air.

I watched with eager eyes, my breath barely rippling the froth on the waves. My hands gripped tight to the moss-coated rocks as my fins were nibbled clean by the tiny fish living in the shoals, poised to escape beneath the depths when the heavens finally crashed down to whip the waves into a frenzy.

I left my leaving long, clinging in place as the air charged and crackled and thunderclouds of a sudden boiled up on the horizon. With a gleeful laugh, I dove deep and fast just before the stormfront blanketed the world above.

None on water or in air saw mercy from that tempest. I came up to the shallows when the worst passed, eager to see the evidence of the storm's might. With care I darted from mass to mass, just beneath the water. All I found was broken by the punch of the waves and wind, bitten by the power of the lightning. Fragments of those odd conveyances rained down, caught and cradled a moment before being swallowed by the sea.

I turned my attention to the masters of those vessels. The bodies I left for the currents to slurp down, or batter upon the distant sands as they may. There was one I came across with warmth yet in his veins. I wrapped both arms around and drew him down with me. Beneath the runnels of blood and scraggled hair there was something of his face that spoke of fear. He jerked and thrashed as the waves closed overhead, his odd, split tail flailing uselessly against my single powerful one. I murmured reassurances in his ear, but he continued to struggle. Grimacing, I tightened my grip and swam more swiftly to gain us the sanctuary of my private grotto.

I held an eager breath. Never had I had this chance before. To speak to one who made their home above the water. One who knew of the sky jellies. I held little if any doubt of communication between us. In my long life I had travelled far and listened well, I was certain I could speak and understand every language the man-things spoke near the sea — which was to say all of them.

I knew what I would ask him. The only thing I cared to ask him: *How? How do you reach the sky?* It was my dearest dream to take my place up there, to gain those distant shores and swim the waters of the unseen moon. I dreamt of dancing with the lightning, of climbing its jagged bolts into the heavens. There were oceans there. I could not see them, but I could feel their call in the shivers down my scales and the tremors through my whisker hairs. I had no doubt those waters were there. After all, look how much spray rained down to mingle here below.

The lightning climbed up into the sky. Those like the one wrapped in my arms rode the winds. Perhaps the air-jellies were the key to gaining the clouds. This one held the secret. He *would* give it up. My egg sibs scoffed, but I would not rest until I was as cradled by those waters above as I was by my own sea.

And here was my chance to discover the secret to making this so.

But my effort was for naught. By the time we shook off the water's clinging, and I drew the stranger from above up upon my own hidden sands deep below, the warmth had fled him. I stared at his peculiar face and my teeth gnashed, jagged edge against jagged edge. I traced the plump curve of his now-blue lips and peered into strange, near-flat eyes, gone blood-shot and lifeless, as if my answers were written there. They were not. But something did glitter slightly lower. I reached out, pushing aside the odd flaps that covered his chest like a skin torn loose and let flop to either side. Beneath was a wonder. It was an object like lightning-struck sand only smooth and straight and clear. Something encapsulated within glowed faintly. I lifted the thing away, breaking the thin strap it hung from around the dead one's neck. And none too soon.

A splash behind me betrayed an intrusion. "Your bottom-feeder tendencies are showing, my dear."

Phin. Like a case of scale rot, that one had plagued me ever since we were fingerlings. Even in the sac he was rotten, I was sure. Someday, when I spawned my young, I would eat any eggs that held darkness such as his, for Phin had one goal: by word and deed, inflict what harm he may and often. His disdainful tone sent my lips into a snarl. As if I would feed upon a thinking being.

Before he spied it, I slipped my prize into the kelp bands I'd strung about my waist for carrying such things as I did not wish to hold in my hands. I then turned and glared at where he lounged, flukes in the water, arms on the sands, bracing him up. As ever, his eyes were mocking.

He could not have noticed my expression.

Not when he was too busy staring up and down the length of me, eyes lingering in the region of my pelvic fins. Hissing with annoyance and distaste, I heaved the strange one to my shoulder. With a wiggle of my fins and tail I shoved past my egg brother—we were sheltered in the same nest, though not spawned from the same source—before sliding into the water, hauling the corpse to the grotto entrance where I let the eager current reclaim its prize.

Unburdened but still weighed down, I undulated upward. The surface was choppy yet, dotted with flotsam not claimed by the depths, but the clouds had vanished as quickly as they'd come, leaving the sky deep and dark and finely speckled like a dolphin. I let my head fall back, eyes closed, and breathed deep of the cleansed, ozone-scented air, savoring the lingering taste of salt water tinged with fresh-churned kelp on my lips. Slowly my muscles unbunched. My eyes opened to scan the sky. To the left, high up, I spied a patch seemingly void of stars. A dark cloud? One of the sky jellies? I could not say, but without a doubt I could dream. With a few powerful strokes of my tail I swam again toward the rocks, hauled myself up and let the moonbeams caress my skin and scales. I looked up to the larger moon, the one all could see. Its touch was cool, soft. Pleasant, but nothing more. The other… the hidden moon… I glowed with the charge it imbued. Warmth bathed me on the inside, despite the chill of the night.

Someday… .Someday I would gain that vaunted moon's shores and swim in its vibrant seas.

Forcing my gaze down and away lest I remain mesmerized for longer than was safe, I looked to the object tucked within my kelp bands. My hand trembled as I drew it out with care. It was fine, more delicate than I would have thought possible. I could imagine neither its purpose nor manner of creation. I had taken it because it caught my eye. I kept it for it seemed a treasure, something of value to the lost soul I had claimed it from. Perhaps it would serve a purpose for me, as lure or boon to one from his world who might aid me. I secured it once more, not wanting the jealous waves to claim my prize.

That was when I heard it. A broken sound. A weak one. It was foreign even to me, who had ventured forth through all the earthly seas available to me—which was to say, all of them. I was a powerful swimmer.

My dorsal fronds stiffened, not quite billowing as they would beneath the waves, but nonetheless they snapped at the air in eager anticipation. This was a new thing. I angled my head to capture the sound. To pinpoint the source. It had something of a seal's bark—were the seal half dead. And something of the seagull's caw, only much less demanding. I could not for a moment imagine what made such a sound. Taut with the need to know, I drew myself across the rocks, up through the crevice that split this oceanic outcrop. I was silent as I moved, the muscles in my tail bunching to push against the rock, aiding my arms as they may. As I drew closer to the sound I slowed my motions. A tall, thin spire of rock jutted high overhead. With care, I placed my webbed fingers against its jagged mass and pulled myself up to peer around the bulk of it.

The water glittered in the moonlight as it could not hope to beneath the sun, else I would not have noticed. An odd form clinging to the base of the outcrop, half in and half out of the waves, broke up that liquid shimmer. It humped first large, then smaller, holding to the rocks as tight as a barnacle did. There was the odd glimmer as the moon stroked something wet and sleek, but only in patches, as if the form were not all of one thing.

I almost lost my grip and tumbled down as suddenly a different, higher wail rose, piercing my delicate ears clear through. And then I saw the one form was two, small huddled against the large. My pelvic fins fluttered instinctually. I watched as the bigger of the two pulled the other close to shelter against her… for her it was, I could see as the moon now caressed the paleness of her face. The little one looked up and a sound escaped me. It was a boy-thing, small lips full and flat eyes familiar, though lacking the tinge of blood red last seen upon the eyes of another face. Were the sea kinder, I could see this one might grow into the man-thing I'd gripped in my arms not long ago.

Perhaps it was my earlier thoughts of spawning, but an ache settled in my chest to see that young one at the mercy of the sea. I leaned closer, my head tilted for a better view, my ear hole bent toward them to pick up the words drifting on the night's breeze.

"He said that he would find us… he promised. If anything happened to the ship," the woman-thing murmured through cracked lips. Her words drifted, broken and as faint as the sounds she'd first made. "Find a place of safety, he said and signal him. He will come. He promised. But the flare… it's gone." Her one hand rose briefly to touch an object around her neck. From a familiar strap hung the fragments of what seemed the cousin to the object hidden in my kelp bands. As the woman-thing slid deeper in the water she scrambled to cling to the rocks once more.

More of the tortured sounds, point and counterpoint, high voice and low. Though the sounds hurt my ears I remained perched in my crevice, oddly captivated by the scene below. As I stayed there, the night air brushed over my form, gentle but persistent, until my skin and scales itched and twitched and tightened enough to bring me to wailing myself. The depths called to me, soothing and wet, cool and dark, and yet I watched until I spied the boy-thing slide into the grip of the waves. The woman-thing cried out and dove fearlessly after, in several long moments surfacing with her sputtering young. He choked and gasped as I have never heard a creature come from the sea. Great wracking coughs spewed water upon the rocks. My gaze went to his neck. I gasped myself and my gills twitched in empathy when realization dawned: as the fish remained ever below, these man-things thrived only above. My mouth gaped with remorse as my eyes opened to what I had done in drawing the man-thing down beneath the waves. I had borne no malice, yet like Phin I'd wreaked great harm. Even could I wrest the man-thing from the sea the deed could not be undone. He would not breathe again, nor return to these steadfastly waiting. But there was one thing I could do in restitution. My numb fingers slid down to grip the rod still lodged within my now-dry kelp bands. It had clearly held import for him, kept, as it was, hidden against his breast. I suspect this was another of the flares the woman-thing worried over.

I knew what I must do.

Sliding back down the outcrop, harsh rock scraping free dried scales as I went, I slipped with a grateful sigh back into the sea. Powerful twitches of my tail sent me around the rocks to where the two I'd watched still clung. From this new vantage point I saw they perched because they could not climb higher against the algae-coated rock. This I could fix. The night air splintered with their shrieks as I braced against their bottoms, first the boy-thing, then the woman-thing, and with powerful thrusts of my tail surged forward, propelling them from the sea and up onto the rocks. They scrambled higher, clutching each other in as tight a grip as I'd held their man-thing when I drew him under the sea. I bobbed there where they had clung, merely watching, bemused but content that the waters would not have them. I met the gaze of the woman-thing, remorse in my eyes, though my tongue remained silent.

I had not the words to make my deed right, none to excuse them. I bowed my head down as I slid my hand into the kelp band, working the object free. It glowed in the moonlight as I brought it forth and the terror in the woman-thing's expression lightened with a gleam of hope. Like a crab, she sidled toward my outstretched hand, snatching my prize and scurrying back.

Without a word I turned away and dropped beneath the waves, but not before I glanced a fleeting moment up into the sky. Someday I would dance with the lightning, and climb its jagged bolts into the heavens. Someday... I would reach those distant shores to swim the seas of the unseen moon.

But not today.

Windows to the Soul

30, October, 1870

> *The crows are what I remember most clearly of the day they say my father died. They wheeled in the sky, a black whirlwind of feathers, beaks, and talons, dipping and diving over the remains of Papa's cherished courtyard. They screamed their outrage. My heart cried with them, though my voice remained mute, shocked at the destruction that surrounded me. I had turned a slow circle before dropping to my knees at the center of what had recently been a garden oasis once tended by my mother's gentle hand. It lay in ruins around me, rose bushes torn from the ground, their petals bruised and stained, and other flowers, for which I did not even have names, had been crushed into the dirt. The fountain at the heart of the garden lay toppled and shattered while blood marred the white marble cobblestones beneath me. But of my beloved Papa... there was no sign.*

> *A.A.F*

Aleta Angelina Fabricio set down her quill, her hand only slightly trembling. It had been many months, but not until now had she found the strength to document what she had seen. It hardly seemed necessary, the memories were so crisp, but she could not risk overlooking anything. All Saints' Day drew near, and with it, Día de Muertos—the Day of the Dead. If there was any time to prove what she suspected, it was now.

No matter what she had been told, she would not believe that her father was dead when she had cause to doubt. No body had ever been found. And a month ago, on a rare trip into nearby Oaxaca, Lina was certain she had seen him in the distance, though he had gone before she reached where she thought he had been. There were other times she would swear she had seen him, but none as certain as that day. She could not say what kept him away from his family, but she could use a device of his own creation to prove it was not death.

Before his… *disappearance*… Papa had been working on his grand invention, one Lina hoped to adapt. The original intent was to grant the wearer the ability to part the Veil between life and death, to see beyond the physical world into that of the afterlife. In his journal, Papa had claimed to have finally achieved success. However, if he had, Lina could not say. Above his worktable, there were two boxes, one empty, the other containing only a partially constructed device. Her father was always meticulous in documenting his process. Using his journal, it should be a small matter to complete his work. Lina prayed that was so and that she knew enough to put practice to his theory.

Setting aside her journal, she drew her father's to her. The pages were filled with diagrams drawn in a fine hand in clear and intricate detail. Surrounding the images were meticulous notations, but also amongst them tender passages giving insight to what drove him. The pain. The longing. The love. She read of aether and lenses and windows to the soul… that was how he put it. So poetic. His grand plan. Her mother had been the other half of his heart. His soul. And he had been determined to look upon her once more, and the son lost with her. To know that even death did not part them. Lina frowned. He had been so focused on that goal that Lina herself may as well have been a ghost, for all he saw her, always there, always tending to his needs, never noticed.

Faint bitterness bit at the back of her throat. Early on, when she was younger, it would have festered, but as an adult, she forced it away. Even had she not read his journal, she would have known the love her father had for his family, including her. If Mother had not died so suddenly, without warning… The loss had been terrible, leaving Father half a man and that half driven to be whole again. Love for him kept Lina rereading long into the night. Checking and rechecking the science of his work, making sure she fully understood before she took his watchmaker's tools to the delicate machinery half-finished in its box above his worktable. Her eyes burned from reading and she had already filled the lantern twice over.

Closing her eyes, she massaged her scalp where she had pinned back her dark locks to keep them out of her way. Behind her Papa's pet crow Beltran gave a broken croak. She rose and went to him, careful to make a *shh*ing sound to announce her presence lest the bird startle and bring his beak against her. Slowly, gently she ruffled his crest, as Father used to do. She marveled at how the feathers felt both soft and slick to her touch. The crow made low moan-like sounds and leaned into her fingers.

Faithful Beltran. She had found him beneath the remains of her mother's favorite rose bush, battered and near to death, his eyes gouged from his head. Lina marveled that he still lived, regardless of her efforts. Her heart broke to see the still-angry red lines of scars layering his face, bald of feathers around the sockets where his eyes had been. Somehow she had restored his health. Now to restore his vision. Beltran was the key, if her father's notations were correct, for many believed that crows possessed the gift of seeing into both worlds, that of the living and the dead. This was the crux of her father's premise.

In a box beside the crow's perch lay a brass cowl the size of a child's bracelet or a large man's ring but bent slightly outward, thin, with wires and ocular lenses suspended in the center. Next to that was a small bottle of laudanum. The traveling doctor had given it to Lina weeks after that day in the garden to aid her rest. The nightmares had been relentless. They still were for she would not drug herself, not at the risk of dimming her thoughts and disassociating herself from the world, not when she depended on the sharpness of her mind more now than ever. She suffered the pain of those dreams for they drove her to success here in her father's workroom.

"Are you ready, pequeño?" *Little one.*

On his perch, Beltran bobbed up and down and ruffled his feathers before settling once more. Lina stroked down his back, not certain if she was soothing herself or the bird. The premise of what she was about to attempt had been outlined in her father's journal in precise detail. She had grown up at his side, observing, if not helping, in this very room on one invention or another. Nothing of what he wrote was beyond her. Drawing a deep breath and releasing it slowly, she first moved to the washbasin and cleaned her hands. Then she dusted the work area carefully, capturing any dirt on a cloth before taking out the folding pouch containing Papa's prized tools. Unrolling the canvas, she set it to the side within easy reach then took down from the shelf above her head a wooden box edged in brass plates studded with rivets. As she opened it her breath caught in her chest. She smelled the faint musk of oiled leather as the lantern light glimmered off of a set of intricate goggles. The lenses shimmered silver with faintly rainbow-hued swirls. In truth, they were dual lenses of clear polished glass. The tint came from the gas trapped between them. Her father called it aether and claimed it the substance of the beyond. How he had captured a sampling was and always would be a mystery to her. Attached to one of those lenses inside the leather frame of the goggles was a fine filament of copper wire that ended in webbing adhered to the thinnest of curved glass plates Lina had ever seen. Here she shuddered faintly before steeling herself. Per her father's notations, that minute disc must be applied direct onto her eye, but only one of them, else her vision would be completely filled with the afterlife, blinding her to the mortal realm around her.

Beltan's cowl was of the same design, now minus their even smaller curved discs. Lina had removed them, given his lack of eyes. She only hoped that the wires themselves set into the sockets where the crow's eyes had been would function the same. If any remnant of the nerves remained, there was hope.

"Aleta Angelina Fabricio!"

Lina jerked around, catching the edge of her lip between her teeth as she met her grandmother's eye. She forced her head to remain level, rather than dipping in instinctive guilt at the use of her full name.

"Yes, Abuela?"

"You promised me you would sleep, and yet here I find you in this infernal workroom," Grandmother said, with a disapproving *hmph* at the end, as she drew her shawl tighter about her shoulders. Lina frowned as she noticed how threadbare the nightgown beneath it was. "It is nearly dawn, child. If you have no care for yourself, do you not at least remember you are to help me with the ofrenda in the morning?"

"Yes, Abuela," Lina answered respectfully, but with no intention of going to her rest. There was no time, which her grandmother had just served to remind her. Besides, she exaggerated. The clock above the door read barely one.

"Ay Dios mio! You are as bad as your father. I know you will do as you please. Just like Vasco. And you see where that got him…"

Lina's jaw clenched at that, for even were she to believe her father dead, she would *not* believe it any fault of his own. And for her grandmother to say so… Forcing her expression to relax she walked to her mother's mother and placed a kiss on her weathered cheek, while smoothing a hand over her silver-shot braid as she had Beltran's feathers.

"I am sorry, Abuela. I am almost done. I will go to bed shortly."

31, October, 1870

I do not know why Abuela pushes me to sleep. It never ends well. I am better rested by closing my eyes throughout the day, as I am wont to do, than to subject myself to the nightmares. This night it was the vision of a skeletal dog. No. More wolf or coyote than dog. Fur hung from its bones and the eyes burned like coals in a brazier. All of it was weathered and aged but for the teeth, which gleamed sharp and bright to my sleeping eye. Rising from it was the musty scent of the grave and the metallic tang of spilt blood. Beyond the beast stood a shadow without the form of a man, but with the feel of one. It watched intently as the canid hounded me, chasing me through a graveyard full of souls, past families feasting at altars with their deceased loved ones. I woke just as I was forced below to the realm of Mictlan, of which my Abuela often tells tales, the underworld of her Aztec ancestors. Tales where the spirits of the dead journeyed the underworld with dog-companions. I woke choking on screams this morning feeling the phantom slice of wind-blown knives shredding my flesh while at my back a jaguar snarled, about to devour my unworthy soul. I may never sleep again.

A.A.F.

By the time Lina left her room in the morning, her grandmother had already pulled the bare ofrenda into its place in the central room of their hacienda, not above using what was convenient even while she derided the memory of the one responsible for its making. Lina's Papa built the altar, simple, but ingenious, made to be sturdy. Made to be as easily raised up as folded down and stored for the next year. They had been using it a long time. This year Lina would watch to see if Papa came to feast from his own table. Her heart could not believe he would.

Her grandmother's disapproving look followed Lina as she shuffled from her room and into the kitchen. On the back of the cast-iron stove a pot of frijoles simmered. The rich scent of garlic and onion and chili caused her gorge to rise. Breathing shallow and swallowing hard, Lina quickly prepared herself a cup of willow bark tea heavily laced with honey. Grit burned in her eyes and her head ached, feeling tight, as if the demons of her nightmare hung from her hair. She said nothing of this. To what end? Abuela would never give credence or sympathy when she was fully confident she already knew the cause of Lina's discomfort.

"Good morning, Abuela," she said as she hugged her grandmother.

"*Hmph*. Nearly noon."

By the sun coming through the window it could be no later than nine o'clock. Lina again said nothing, merely moving past her to the leather-banded chest against the wall, lid open and waiting. "The papel picado are looking a little faded. Shall we make new or use these another year?" she asked her grandmother as she shifted the paper banners to the side to lift the snowy-white altar cloth from the chest.

Abuela sniffed. "No time. We've the calavera de azucar to finish."

Lina had always loved decorating the little sugar skulls, so bright and festive and full of love. This year she had no heart for it, though she knew she must. As they sat at the table in the kitchen she dutifully drew flowers and swirls and crosses in colorful icing on the glittery skulls her grandmother had molded. Upon each one she wrote the names of those loved ones past: Angelina for her mother, after whom she was named; Maximo for her baby brother, who never had drawn breath; Tio Luis and Tia Lucia, her mother's siblings, who died as children.

On one, Abuela wrote in her shaky hand "Papi Orlando" for Lina's grandfather.

Finally, one skull remained. Lina drew it to her, staring overlong into those empty eye sockets and the cheerful toothy grin. This one was meant for her father. Carefully, in golden hue, she iced the skull using the approximation of gears in place of flowers and spanners in place of a cross, because it would have made him smile. That was as far as she could bring herself, though Abuela waited expectantly, her brow drawing down the longer Lina hesitated.

"Well? There is work to be done beyond this."

"I am sorry, Abuela," Lina answered with the quickness of habit. As she stared at the almost-finished skull she reminded herself that the names written upon them were not always those of the dead. With that she was able to scribe her father's name, Vasco, in good faith. She set the skull aside and finished helping her grandmother decorate the altar.

From the other room, Beltran cawed stridently.

1, November, 1870

I am better rested from a siesta spent only in part napping on the cot in Papa's workroom, than I was after most of a night in my own bed. Though I must confess, I spent more time making adjustments to Beltran's cowl and the newly finished goggles, than I did in slumber. I do believe I am more intimately familiar with Papa's device than even he is. After, I joined Abuela in the courtyard, where she gathered the flor de muerto. The marigolds grew large and well, despite the near destruction of the garden mere months ago, bright and golden and pungent in their scent, surely fragrant enough to guide our beloved spirits home. They are the final decoration we need for the ofrenda, already heavy with sweets, pan de muerto, and, of course, the calaveras. My mouth waters even now at the thought of the sweet bread dipped in a cup of Abuela's rich and spicy chocolate, a special and costly treat only to be had this night. Abuela claims it is her only chance to spoil her grandson, who she never held, but she always looks at me with particular fondness when she says so. While Abuela was at her work I examined the fountain, the sole aspect of the courtyard so far beyond my means to fix. I was startled to find among the rubble a torn piece of leather strap, brass-riveted and distinctly familiar. This very day I attached its cousin to the goggles stored on my father's shelf.

A.A.F.

The scent of crushed herbs, spices, and roasting meat filled the hacienda, enticing Lina's appetite as Abuela cooked her younger children's favorite meal. The aroma mingled with the rich heavy perfume of burning copal resin tempered by the sweetness of the beeswax altar candles. Their family, in the old tradition, observed Dia de los Inocentes in the privacy of their own home, out of respect for the little ones lost too young to know any but their family or, like Maximo, did not get to dance with life at all. Tomorrow night, Día de Muertos, she and Abuela would trek to the nearby graveyard to celebrate the adults at the family plot, as most did.

Lina's thoughts lingered on Maximo. She had only ever known the thought of him, but she held a deep love for her brother in her heart and had often as a girl made up tales to tell her father, stories of her adventures with Maximo. What he looked like and things they had done. Though Papa had laughed or showed proper awe, as was fitting to the tale, all the while the hint of tears glimmered in his eyes. For Dia de los Inocentes, they had always built something special as a gift for him. In the workroom an entire shelf held the tinkered offerings from past years, kept carefully dusted.

Earlier that night Lina had placed on the altar a tiny steam-powered wagon. The first gift she'd built alone.

Tears glimmered in her own eyes when she imagined she heard Maximo's laughter as he played.

The echo of that sound tempted her to fetch Beltran and the goggles from the workroom, only to do so—on this holy day in particular— would bring down Abuela's wrath. She loathed the bird and would not countenance him in her home, anywhere beyond the workroom. (At times when her patience was worn thin, Lina had to restrain herself from pointing out this home belonged to Vasco Fabricio, *not* Aleta Cuacuas.) Just as well; part of her feared to test Papa's invention too soon, as if to do so would rob her of the chance for which she so desperately held out hope. Tomorrow she would don the goggles, during the trek to the graveyard where the spirits mingled with the living at public altars, and none would notice one more crow, no matter how unusual.

To distract herself, Lina murmured stories of their father to Maximo.

That night Lina paced her room as a coyote's howl mocked her from the darkness beyond the courtyard wall. Even without the mournful sound, she felt anxious… by some means watched, the shadows on her wall looming in menace. With the howls reminding her of her nightmares there was no hope of sleep. She sighed and crept from her bedchamber to her father's workroom as quiet as she could. Once there she draped a thick canvas—sporting burns and nicks and other testaments to its service—over the doorframe to block any sign of the lantern light that might betray her. She then crossed to the perch where Beltran rested, his cowl still in place. She would have thought it uncomfortable, but earlier when she had attempted to remove the mechanism the crow had resisted. She ran a light finger over the glossy feathers along his neck before pouring some seeds and nuts into the bowl beside his perch. He stirred and looked up at her through faintly red-tinged lenses before ruffling his feathers and settling to rest once more.

Smiling, she took a carved wood mask from the cabinet below him. It was smooth and contoured beneath her touch, shaped as a sugar skull, but lacking any color. Though such masks were traditional, a means of mocking death and robbing that specter of any power to be gained through fear, this was the first year Lina had thought to wear one. She wasn't sure why, maybe it was the nightmares, or maybe she felt the need for courage as she tested her belief… in either case, until now she had been undecided, though earlier she had made a makeshift scythe from a shoulder-high walking stick and a blade of tin from among Papa's scrap pile, in honor of Santa Muerte.

Taking out the paints she and her father had used for Maximo's various gifts, she began to decorate the mask. While the symbols of the *calaveras* took shape, flowers and filigree, intermixed with the gears and tools of her inventor's trade, in her thoughts she sent a prayer to the Saint of Death, also called the Lady of Shadows, petitioning for her protection.

Whether for herself or for her father, Lina could not say.

2, November, 1870

> *I do not know which fills me with the most dread. The thought that I will see my father tonight, or the thought that I will not.*

A.A.F

The light of a thousand candles glowed in the twilight. Perched upon gravestones, nestled among flowers, held in the hands of those walking among the plots. Illuminating *calaveras*, portraits of lost loved ones, the joyous faces of the living, families celebrating everywhere, disturbingly like the memory of her nightmares. Lina shivered and continued on. Bright marigold petals sprinkled the flagstone path she followed. The dizzying scents of rich food and incense filled the air as quiet laughter and conversation came to Lina's ear. It was late and she walked alone, her right hand holding her scythe while a basket of pan de muertos, roasted goat, and huevos con nopales hung over her other arm. When it had been time to leave she and her grandmother had fought over Lina's manner of dress—calaveras mask, a faded blue cotton robe, goggles perched atop her head like a diadem—and Beltran on her right shoulder with his metal cowl. Though she regretted upsetting her grandmother, Lina had remained steadfast, earning Abuela's ire. In the end, her mother's mother refused to come.

Lina put that from her mind as she looked ahead to her goal. She stopped in the shadow of a monument, leaning her scythe against the stone and setting her basket on the ground to slide the goggles down into place over the mask, fumbling a moment as she placed the thin glass disc on the surface of her right eye. The cold, hard sensation caused her to flinch. It was an effort not to blink furiously, sending the disc fluttering aside, but she managed.

As she looked through the aether lenses Aleta Angelina Fabricio gasped.

Slowly she turned a full circle, letting her gaze trail over the family gatherings.

It worked.

Papa's invention worked!

Through her left eye, with her mortal vision, Lina saw the family groupings as they were, but through her right eye she saw additional guests seated at those feasts. Flickering and translucent, the spirits silently laughed or smiled or occasionally looked on in faint disappointment as they breathed deep, drawing their sustenance from the heady steam wafting from the warm meals prepared for their enjoyment, as if perhaps the dish made had not in truth been their favorite.

She laughed with their success—hers and her father's—though the split vision made her sway and almost stumble as she gathered her things and continued on. Occasionally, she had to stop as Beltran looked elsewhere and half her vision diverged from what was before her. She was glad of her walking-stick scythe as she traveled through the graveyard. Still, her hope blossomed a bit more with each step.

Nowhere she looked did she see her father. Surely she would have, were he dead.

Lina could not say if it was nerves or excitement that clenched in her belly, but as she approached her parents' graves she reached up and caressed Beltran's wing. At her touch he turned and groomed a bit of her hair with his beak, oddly comforting. But even as she drew her hand away, the crow tensed, then mantled, crying out the harshest caw she had ever heard him utter. Jerking, she looked up but could see no reason for his anger.

She did notice, though, that at some point Abuela must have come down to the gravesite to set up an altar, beautifully arranged, with a silver-backed mirror propped against the headstone to reflect the candlelight. If it held more tribute to Lina's mother than her father, well... if Abuela could not be forgiven her bias, at least it was understood.

Just before Lina reached the altar someone stepped onto the path before her, blocking her way.

Beltran continued to scream from her shoulder, fluttering violently.

Lina gasped again as she peered at the shadow before her. The looming form served as another echo of her nightmares. It stood there without the form of a man, but the feel of one. Shaking her head as if to clear it, she swayed and blinked, first closing her right eye, then her left. With her left eye open what stood before her was clearly a living, breathing man—a man with her father's face! But with her right eye, a gleam encased him, as if spirit and body were not one. With either eye the malice in his expression shone clear.

The man/not-man before her was unnatural. His very presence a menace to more than just herself, or so she suspected. It made no sense to her. But however this being stole her father's body, Lina believed it had happened that fateful day in the courtyard. Was it a spirit? A demon? She doubted she would ever know for certain, the what, the how, or the why of it. What she did know was she must stop him.

Tension burned like a firebrand through her. On instinct, she dropped the basket, but took a firmer grip on the scythe. The blade held no edge, but the stick was solid and long.

"You meddle where you shouldn't, girl. This vessel is mine now."

Then, the man that was and was not her father drew a *tecpatl* from his coat, the obsidian blade gleaming black on black in the darkness. As he raised the sacrificial knife he sneered at her.

"When you reach the Underworld, tell Xolotl I won't be coming back. I have no wish to test my... 'worthiness' in the realm of Mictlan, when there is power yet to be had here in the Overworld. I will make this world mine to rule."

Even the voice differed from Papa's.

As he brought the blade down toward her chest he darted his other hand forward to snatch Beltran from her shoulder, his motions strangely careful, as if he dare not harm the crow. Lina brought up the scythe to block him, forcing him away before he could succeed. With the way clear before her, her gaze fell full on the mirror.

The breath went out of her.

In the glass she saw her own reflection, but at her back, seemingly against her right shoulder, where Beltran should have been, stood her father's spirit. Thin threads — like the wires attaching the lens she wore to the goggles — ran from the reflection of her father to his body. Lina moaned as she realized part of how her attacker bore Papa's face, but not his soul. And why he had tried to capture the crow.

Her father spoke to her, distracting her from her thoughts, the movement of his lip vehement but his words silent. In perfect synchronization with his actions, Beltran's wings clearly beat against Lina's head.

"What?" she cried. "I don't understand."

His efforts in the reflection grew more frantic as the not-him… the physical form lurched toward her, blade raised once more. At his side stalked the spirit of a canid, looking more coyote than dog. As with her father, it yipped and growled in silence but, being purely a spirit, she did not believe it could harm her. Its attention, however, seemed intent not on her, but on Beltran… on her father's shade.

Not knowing what the hound could or could not do to him, Lina gripped the scythe with both hands, her left hand a foot from the blade and the right midway to the butt. Intent on defending her father, she braced herself with care as her vision still threatened to unbalance her.

All of them stilled for but a breath, Lina, the crow, the canid, and the reflections of her father. She looked from the ethereal threads to Papa's spirit, her grip white-knuckled on the scythe.

This time he carefully mouthed his words, "It is the only way, mija, nothing else will stop him."

Even as the demon brought his knife blade down toward her, Lina could not bring herself to move. Then, out of nowhere — or perhaps out of the aether — a woman's voice, hollow and beautiful and unworldly all at once, spoke to her, like a gentle whisper, somehow sounding in her ear and her heart both at once.

"You must."

Sobbing as she listened to Death, Lina's hands clenched tighter on the haft before she let go with her right hand. She lifted the head of her scythe with her left hand and brought the "blade" slicing away from her through the space beside her right shoulder, breaking the threads still linking her father's spirit to his physical form. At the same time, she brought her right hand up to cradle Beltran's body before it could fall. Behind her came the sharp sound of the obsidian blade shattering against flagstones, followed by the thud of a body falling to earth.

An angry, tortured scream echoed in her head, fading quickly to nothing.

Lina barely noticed. As the life went out of the crow she cradled, she looked up into the silver-backed glass. Despite the tears streaming down her face she saw clearly before her a double image, her own skull mask and coarse robe mirrored by a stately figure in need of no mask, wearing rich robes of soft blue velvet. Their scythes overlapped until Lina could not tell one from the other.

The Lady of Shadows reached out and brushed her hand across the crown of Lina's head, as if in benediction, before stepping back among the spirits behind her. To Lina, it appeared she left without her scythe. She wondered at that until she realized what the mirror now reflected.

Beneath Santa Muerte's draped arm stood Vasco Fabricio, faint and shimmery, but unmistakable; beside him stood Lina's mother, her expression both proud and joyous. But between them… between them stood a small boy with Papa's eyes and Mama's smile. Maximo, looking exactly as Lina had always pictured him, though he'd never had the chance to grow so big. Her heart swelled with the love that shone in all four gazes. A part of her wondered how she could still see them without the aid of Beltran's vision. The rest of her didn't care as it drank in the sight.

She smiled back through her tears as the spirits waved farewell.

As all four faded from her sight, Lina acknowledged the lesson her father had hard learned as both blessing and curse: Opening the windows of the soul could let things through from either side.

On The Wings of An Angel

CAN'T SAY AS I DIDN'T RECKON I WAS GOING MAD. IT WOULDN'T HAVE surprised me if'n it were so. I already reckoned I was in hell, that's enough to turn anyone's mind…

But first, I call myself Miss Sadie Angelina Carlisle, though I don't bother much with any name but the middle one anymore. Not since takin' up residence at the Lucky Strike Saloon in Dead Dog, Montana, anyway. See, the proprietor, Mr. Clayton, he says men are happier pretendin' they're keepin' company with an angel, rather than a common whore. I do as I'm told, else Mr. Clayton might forget he likes havin' an angel below stairs temptin' and teasin' the custom, rather than just another girl entertainin' above stairs. Men don't pay near so much for common. They have to save up for an angel, even a fallen one; unless they hit a strike. That ain't happened yet. Till then, I sing.

"Sadie! Sun's settin', quit wool-gatherin' and get yourself into your rig afore I find someone else as fits it!"

Lordie, but that black-hearted Clayton can bellow. I can't help but shudder at his bald-faced threat though. That happen, and I might as well drop the name Angel too. Ain't none of us outta reach of his temper. I'd do to remember that. And I reckon he's been givin' me looks makin' me wonder will I be below stairs much longer anyhow. Looks that make me think he's tired of waitin' for a prospector with that big strike to come along. I've no doubt I've only been spared entertainin' the custom 'cause there ain't anyone come in able to pay the price Mr. Clayton has set on my innocence.

I flinch at the thought and rush to do as I'm bid, my mind near jibberin' half-formed pleas for deliverance, but not hardly expectin' it will ever come. I'm already wearin' my white satin gown and matchin' slippers with the thick leather soles; now for the rest. Quick-like I beckon over Shelby, one of the above stairs ladies, for some help 'cause I plum can't suit up all myself.

See, our Mr. Clayton, he's into mods and mechanicals. Show him somethin' with gears and I reckon he starts breathin' like he's been with a five-dollar whore. There are bits of invention all over the saloon I can scarce make sense of. They're most nothin' much but tinker's toys like the little metal birds what can't fly, but sing pertier than me... if'n only ever just one song, and miniature carriages made for Cook's son movin' by themselves on tiny puffs of steam... .The bartender is flesh enough, but there ain't a bottle of liquor to be seen — nor broke, if'n the custom gets rowdy. Drinks is portioned out by a clockwork contraption of gears and pipes that can take a dent and keep on pourin' the next drink in just as precise a measure as the last. Then there's the player piano what plays itself like any other, but ain't no crank involved, just lotsa steam and valves and whatnot. It's an amazin' thing of copper and brass instead of wood, with gold-plated keys, and not soundin' no more tinny than any other upright I ever heard.

But all of that ain't nothin' compared to my rig.

I can't help but think about that with longin' and loathin' mixed, rememberin' when and how it came to be. There were a tinker come through town. An odd, dirt-smudged, little man what made me more nervous than an uncooped hen after dark. The first he scurried into the saloon and looked his fill at every one of us, we felt near stripped bare down to our very souls, though there weren't nothin' to it that was lecherous or mean. More like Mr. Edward S. Curtis, what came through with his pho-tography equipment once on his way to visit the Blackfoot injuns; he used to look just so at near everythin', like he was searchin' for the perfect picture it would make.

I swear if I didn't feel the tinker's gaze linger just the same on me, though I can't fathom why. I was a young'n yet at the time, and nothin' special to catch the custom's eye. Like now, I sang for my place, when I weren't cleanin'.

Was the tinker first called me Angel, with a nervous-makin' gleam in his eye — like he saw more to me than I right knew was there — and him not even knowin' my given name. That amused Mr. Clayton so much it stuck.

Then that there tinker set to catch Mr. Clayton's attention with such contraptions as you can't never imagine and I can scarce describe. The things that came out of his sack... my Lord, it was a sight. The two of 'em spent more'n a piece of time with their heads together, hagglin'. Hard to say who hoodwinked who, but both men walked away with a smarmy smile.

The tinker stayed a spell after. He puttered around in the cellar until near all you heard afore hours was bangin' and the hiss of steam, but evenin's he ended up in the saloon pesterin' me. Askin' questions and starin' me up and down mutterin' "not yet" under his breath, like maybe I didn't quite match the picture in his head.

The questions made me more nervous than the mutterin'. They was dangerous questions: *What did I wish for? What would I rather be?* I was too feared then to speak, but my heart... it was cryin' out to be free! There was nothin' I wanted more than deliverance. The tinker just nodded and gave me a wink, like he heard what I ain't said, before disappearin' again back down to the cellar.

I wanted to believe. Darn near convinced myself he could do anythin'—includin' save me—after seein' him tinker with one of the songbirds what always sang particularly sad. I'd felt my forehead for a fever when he closed up its tiny back and brushed a finger over it what set it glitterin' and glowin' like pixie dust. Then... that little bird took wing, flyin' out the window never again to be seen! It trilled a happy song as it escaped.

A *different* song.

That's when I had to wonder was I goin' mad.

And still, I took to hopin' then, though ain't nothin' ever come of it.

Afore he left for good, that little man cornered me in the pantry whiles I was helpin' Cook with supper. He stood there, hunched and taut, again starin' me up and down all familiar-like. "Don't you worry... for now, you're safer here," he'd murmured, his head side-cocked and his eyes narrowed like he was lookin' again for his own perfect picture. "But remember, when that's no longer so... Angels were made to fly."

His words left me ashiver in a way I declare I'd never felt afore or since.

To this day, I can hear him whisperin' that, and would swear on my dead ma's Bible if'n I had it that I sometimes still spy him in the shadows, watchin', eyes narrowed just so, though I know he's gone. Quite mad, true, I but can't help but wishin' that mayhap the tinker were right and I'll have me a chance to fly away.

Anyhow, by the time the tinker finally moved along after considerable time spent in the cellar, the parlor had acquired somethin' wondrous new.

Even now I can't help but hold my breath whiles Shelby unlocks my special cabinet. The thing is tall, clear up to the above stairs ceilin'. The whole front and sides foldin' back with fancy paintin' everywhere on the inside, like you would imagine heaven to be, all but for what Mr. Clayton calls the new-matic tube; a brass pipe runnin' down the center, shiny as the day the tinker set it in place.

My rig just hangs there in the middle of the air like someone forgot to paint in the angel, 'ceptin' for its halo and wings—I ain't ever yet been tall enough for that halo to perch proper atop my head. Each time I see The Angel it dazzles me, so's I always near forget how much I dread to buckle the contraption on.

Ain't got no choice, though. Never did. Mr. Clayton says an Angel's gotta have wings if'n anyone's gonna believe she fell from heaven.

An' mayhap they do, when I'm singin'—if I can be forgiven the smallest bit of pride. Savin' for my voice, there's precious little about me that ain't common, or so my pa use to say. 'Course given this rig here—and the presence of the above stairs ladies—I'd be a mite surprised did the gents notice a thing about myself, no matter that I'm hoverin' in thin air above their heads lookin' near the picture of angelic. (Times like that, I can't help but remember the tinker's words… and that little metal songbird. My heart goes all tight each time I do…)

Oh glory, just to look at it… . Wings made of gen-u-ine swan feathers brushed light like with gold. Mr. Clayton's after callin' it *guilt*, then laughin' his fool ass off like'n he said somethin' funny. Which, given the nature of his establishment…

I'm mighty fond of those perty wings. The corset, though… that there's a pure torment to wear. I must stand just so the entire time if'n I'm to have enough air to breathe, let alone sing as I'm expected. I do imagine were not the whole thing latched on to the new-matic tube I *could* plum fly away. I reckon I wish that were so somethin' fierce.

Right now, the only thing protectin' my virtue is my singin', and my not-quite-generous curves. I'm afeared that won't be so for long bein' I've had to dodge more'n a few grabbin' hands of late.

Before Mr. Clayton can bellow once more, I step up onto the platform makin' up the bottom of the cabinet, and though I mostly feel forsaken, I lift up a prayer to the God my ma once swore by. After all, in a manner, she'd been delivered, even if her passin' had left me to bear pa alone, if'n only for a short spell, before he foisted me off on Mr. Clayton.

I step into the frame, careful of the many danglin' straps and buckles, makin' sure my feet set just so on the narrow brass plate they're meant to perch on. I shudder to recall the time they'd slipped from that square. The breath was near squeezed out of me. I've learned to be particular since. My eyes close all on their own and I draw deep and full till my lungs near want to burst as Shelby cages me in that rig of iron ribbin', white leather, and polished brass. Otherwise there ain't no room to breathe once the contraption's buckled tight.

Those lookin' on see nothin' but perty; from the moment I'm buckled in till they free me, I'm nigh in pain, forced to stand straight and still as Sundy service else scald my back on the gleamin' brass pole behind me.

It was a wonder I could ever sing a note, but derned if I don't put the nightingale to shame each and every night when I put on The Angel and dangle there in 'heaven' to give the custom a show, and that ain't no boast.

I hear the clunk of the lever bein' pulled across the room, followed by the hiss of steam warmin' the ledge beneath my feet. There's the *whir* of shiftin' gears as the wings spread, and I feel just a bit giddy as I rise up in the air above the platform. Can't help but wonder maybe this time I won't stop in the middle. Mayhap I'll be crushed against the ceilin' or, mayhap I'll sure enough fly away. There ain't no holdin' back my giggle at that. But then the sound of the hiss changes and my perch slows, then stops.

I feel it then. A shiver down m'spine. Familiar-like, enough that I expect I'd see him… the tinker… if'n my eyes weren't shut. I imagine I hear that little songbird as well, and I let my eyes drift open to see did either of 'em really come back.

But all that's there is the familiar sight of The Angel framed in the mirror behind the bar. Only not quite the same as always…

Just a tiny gasp escapes me and I forget to look for what I expected.

For the first time ever, that there halo's just behind my head and The Angel's starin' back, all brown-gold curls and creamy white skin, with a tiny waist and a bosom to put the above stairs ladies to shame. She's wearin' my face.

But it ain't that what startles me. It were Mr. Clayton holdin' up a walnut-size nugget of gold with a shit-eatin' grin on his face. Standin' next to him was a grubby, overlarge miner smellin' rank even from here.

No longer able to deny my days of bein' safe were done, I recoil, only to have fierce heat sear my back.

I don't smell scorched satin or burnt flesh, as I'd expect. I smell a garden like my ma use to have, and again I hear that tiny metal bird. The burnin's gone afore I even draw breath to cry out and in the mirror I swear that pipin' hot brass ain't at my back no more.

A gasp rises from every throat in the room and if I weren't so scared I'd laugh as their eyes go wide, but I'm afraid to move, afraid to fall. Then somethin' brushes my shoulders, sends them tinglin' like they been long asleep and only just wakin' up. I start to glitter. I shiver again and a flush steals over me. Wisps of steam curl at my feet like soft white clouds, no longer overwarm. Then… quiet by my ear, barely louder'n a breath… I hear the tinker's sigh-like whisper, "Now… be free."

I feel like I imagine that bird did, afraid to believe… afraid not to.

My body shakes at the tinker's words, in eager like tremors from head to toe. Mayhap I imagine it… mayhap I truly am mad… but somethin' sparks off my skin, rises up from my bones and sets me aglow. I remember the songbird as I feel the sudden flex of wings at my back, the bunchin' of muscles I ain't ever used. I open my mouth and out pours a terrible, wonderful, glorious sound.

As The Angel sings, the buckles fall away, and m'iron cage rains to the sawdust-covered floor in pieces as gilded feathers lift me to the sky.

Echoes of the Divine

A PALL HUNG OVER CHADSWORTH MANOR, HEAVY AND BROODING, NOT unlike those fraught days when she—Lady Claramina Evangelista Langstrom (nee Pemberton), had managed the estate, if for a vastly different reason. Leaning forward, Clara frowned, peering through the steam-carriage window as they approached. But for the grim air, the grounds were much better maintained than she had ever had the wherewithal to manage. With one glaring exception. She shuddered as the scorched husk of Dthe carriage house—where once Fritz had lived and worked tirelessly on his inventions at her behest—came into view, emerging like a specter from the steam expressed by their engine. Despite the damage being nearly a year old, her nostrils pinched at the faint, bitter tang of burnt wood and metal.

She started as a firm hand came to rest lightly on her arm. Glancing that way, her brow furrowed as she met her husband's worried gaze. "Settle back, love," he murmured. "We'll be there soon enough."

She quirked her lips in a faint grin, a deplorable habit she had acquired from her "coarse American." "We'd be there already if you had let me drive."

A look of mock horror transformed Fritz's expression, swiftly sliding away at her laughter, which broke forth despite her heavy heart.

Only then acquiescing, Clara sat back properly against the cushions and rested her head on Fritz's shoulder. "I am afraid we will find things not at all well."

Fritz brought up his other hand to brush her cheek, catching a tear she had barely noted shedding. "Healing takes time. So does adjusting."

She shuddered. "I can't imagine." Not completely true, thus the very purpose of their visit, to find some way to make amends. Well, *her* purpose, anyway.

Again, she leaned forward, her gaze going to the manor house looming larger ahead the closer they drew. "Will they even welcome us?"

Fritz's sigh stirred the tendrils at the nape of her neck. "I want to say, of course, but we'd best prepare ourselves, just in case. What happened was most tragic, and some measure of responsibility lies with me."

Clara turned sharply, ready to protest but fell silent as Fritz held up his hand and continued, "It does. I left so much of potential hazard behind, unthinking. Who can say if that will count against us?"

She looked away, unable to answer.

As their steam-carriage chugged to a stop at the forecourt before the manor house, Doyle, the driver, disembarked to assist them. Clara drew a quavering breath. Once Doyle opened the carriage door and lowered the step, Fritz descended first and guided her down.

"I am glad we left Sadie Rae with Charles for now," she murmured just loud enough for her husband's ear before straightening her shoulders and assuming the prim demeanor of a gentrified lady. Fritz offered her his arm as Doyle preceded them to knock at the door. The sound echoed, hollow and ominous, before trailing off into prolonged silence. They stood before the door for fifteen minutes or more, patiently waiting, Clara clinging to a fading hope as Fritz stood a stalwart buffer beside her.

"Shall I knock again, madame?" Doyle asked as he set the last of their baggage beside them on the flagstones.

Clara's heart clenched, afraid to say yes, unable to say no.

Before she could answer, the faint sound of footsteps came to her ear. She nearly gasped as the door opened, revealing her cousin, Rockford, Lord Chadsworth himself, looking impeccable to all outward appearances but as hollow on the inside as the knock that had summoned him. With a dour glance and not a word spoken, he turned and walked away, leaving the door ajar.

Vaguely, Clara heard Fritz instruct Doyle to take the steam-carriage around to the kitchen courtyard and refill the boiler at the pump. Then, her husband gathered the baggage, offered his arm, and escorted her inside, closing the door behind them. Dark shadows shrouded the foyer, with not a lamp lit, and dust lay a thin film over every surface, the inside of the manor as unkempt as the outside was manicured. Stepping back so Fritz could set down their things, Clara pressed her lips tight and squared her shoulders. That had not been the warmest welcome, but they hadn't been turned away.

"We'll have to leave the bags for now, until Doyle returns," she said, seeing no sign of a servant to take them. "Now, let us see about the state of these affairs."

Followed by her husband, Clara strode with renewed purpose through the vacant corridors, her steps tapping a rapid pace on the marble tiles until she reached the study, the only room on the ground floor indicating even faint signs of life.

"Rockford, where is Mrs. Talliwight? And Farthingham?" she asked as she pushed open the partially closed door. "For that matter, why are there no day servants…" Her words trailed off at the sight of her cousin slouched in his chair. His gaze seemed lost and his manner morose as he stared at the fragmented remains of a familiar violin, central upon his desk. Rockford flinched as she drew a sharp breath, his only reaction to their presence. Clara gripped Fritz's steadying hand as it settled on her shoulder. "Oh, dear." Clara could not help but exclaim. Inside, she feared she might shatter just as thoroughly as the instrument.

The silence grew strained until she nigh gave up on expecting an answer. Eventually Rockford sighed, and slowly straightened, his gaze rising but still not meeting theirs.

"Malcolm…" he said, the word drawing out, "…ran off another nanny. Mrs. Talliwight is upstairs managing his care until I secure a new one. Farthingham has been discharged to deliver the former nanny to her family home in Surrey and has not yet returned."

Guilt etched fissures deep into Clara's heart. Malcolm, Rockford's son and heir, had been both a prodigy and virtuoso on the violin, by the scant age of nine. By the age of eleven, not only had he performed with the Royal Liverpool Philharmonic Orchestra and the Hallé Orchestra at Manchester, but also with the Scottish Orchestra. He had filled the Crystal Palace on more than one occasion, and even been invited to perform at the Royal Albert Hall — though vicious fate had intervened. Clara had been so proud to attend each of his performances. He played with such passion and skill well beyond anything to be expected from one of his tender years.

The sight of his shattered violin, once precious to him… Clara bit her lip until she nearly tasted blood rather than cry out and add to her dear cousin's woes. He had already lost Diana, his beloved wife, at Malcolm's birth. And now, the accident that had gutted the carriage house had gravely injured Malcolm, leaving him with nerve damage in his hands that robbed him of his ability to play. Robbed him of his once glorious future. Rumor speculated that the Royal Philharmonic Society had been about to present him with their coveted Gold Medal for outstanding musicianship, presented to only sixteen musicians since its inception. Unheard of for one so young, and now, forever unrealized.

Perhaps coming to help had not been the right decision.

Rockford drew a deep, settling breath and pushed to his feet, belatedly assuming the proper and polite mien of a lord receiving guests into his home.

"Please, allow me to show you to the library where you can wait while I… have your rooms readied." The pause had been ever so slight, but sufficient for Clara to gather that—in the absence of any household staff—Rockford intended to do the readying himself. He crossed the room and made to direct them, though she needed no guidance.

Clara laid her hand upon his arm. "Rockford… cousin, you have more pressing concerns. Fritz and I can more than manage to open a window and freshen the sheets," she murmured gently, then drew him down to place a kiss on his cheek. "Please, let us disturb you no more. We'll settle ourselves, then I shall relieve Mrs. Talliwight so she can see to dinner."

For a moment, her cousin's eyes held a faint glint, as if tears threatened, then it was gone. He straightened with a slight nod and patted her hand. "Very well, Clara. Thank you."

She smiled, though her heart ached. "We shall see you at dinner."

Rockford smiled back, only slightly forced. "Dinner, then." He waited until they collected their baggage and mounted the stairs to the upper levels before closing his study door.

Dinner was a solemn affair, consisting solely of the Langstroms, Lord Chadsworth, and his son, Malcolm, with Mrs. Talliwight serving. Doyle had taken his meal in the kitchen before retiring to one of the rooms over the stable, and Farthingham had not yet returned from Surrey.

Clara's nephew at first had refused to join them, no matter how she'd tried to persuade him before coming down herself to deliver his regrets. But Rockford, at his breaking point, had ordered the boy from his room using the distance speaker Fritz had installed long ago, when she had been in residence. Clara made every effort to focus her attention on the air bladder in Rockford's hand and not the harsh, strained words it conveyed to a similar bladder upstairs by means of vibrations traveling along a linking wire, but it was nigh impossible not to overhear.

Suffice it to say, Malcolm presented himself for dinner, though clearly unwilling.

He entered the room with stiff strides, his posture rigid. Clara could not help noticing his pallor, though to all appearances he had fully recovered—if not recovered *fully*. Though she had spent the afternoon with him, his gaunt appearance nearly startled a gasp from her. She restrained the impulse and carefully did not glance at his hands, instead offering him a smile, willing all the love in her heart visible in her gaze.

"Aunt Clara," he said, stopping beside her to buss her cheek. To her husband, he tendered a respectful nod. "Uncle Fritz." There were no words for his father as Malcolm took his seat.

Rockford made no comment as he motioned for Mrs. Talliwight to serve. Clara could not help but notice a bleak cast to his subdued expression, faint, but clear to one who knew him as she did. As they each in turn served themselves from the proffered platters, Malcolm remained stiffly upright rather than engaging in the meal, his hands below the table edge. No wonder he was but a shade of his former self.

"Malcolm." Rockford placed his utensils on the table with exaggerated care before turning toward his son. He said nothing else, but his pleading gaze landed upon the boy. Clearly hopeful, Mrs. Talliwight positioned herself at Malcolm's left, a platter of roast beef and potatoes at the ready, the meaty, herbaceous scent wafting tantalizingly from the platter.

His expression hard set and his gaze lowered, Malcolm turned toward the offered food and raised his right hand from his lap. Clara could not help but notice his wince as his fingers gripped the serving fork, or how his hand now shook as he attempted to move a portion to his plate, though it had not before. He succeeded, but his features went taut at the effort, and when he moved to place the fork back on the serving tray it fell from his trembling fingers. His hands fisted and his jaw clenched, the mortification clear in every line of him. A thin edge of white limned his pressed lips, the only sign of his pain. And yet, he reached forward for his water glass with little effort, gripping it loosely and bringing it to his lips with only slight effort.

Clara leaned in toward her nephew and murmured, "May I help?"

Malcolm nodded stiffly, but it was sufficient. She reached for the breadbasket set in the center of the table and drew out a warm, yeasty roll. Splitting it, she took up Malcolm's fork and speared a slice of beef from his plate. Folding the roll around it, as she had seen her husband often do, she held it out to her nephew. For a moment, he just stared, almost as if uncomprehending, but then the hint of a smile graced his lips, and he reached out with all confidence to accept the roll and bring it to his mouth. Without a word, she prepared several more for him, placing them on his plate such that he could easily grip one once he was ready for more. For the first time since they arrived, Rockford smiled as he watched his son eat.

Across the table, Fritz sat forward, his head tilted slightly in the way it did when something curious caught his eye, generally a bit of machination he felt compelled to examine, or a problem his mind leapt to solve. Clara glanced back to Malcolm and spied a brace she had not noticed before, a construct of leather and metal rods circling his wrist and extending up the back of his hand, stopping just shy of his first knuckle. A frown teased her lips. She could not conceive how such a construct was meant to help him. From what she had seen, Malcolm's injury affected fine motor skills and dexterity, with some impact on strength. The brace seemed to offer no more than compression and support. In fact, she would hazard that it caused some hindrance to certain tasks.

Clara startled as Malcolm cleared his throat, looking as if he would set the rest of his roll down, half-eaten. She flushed, realizing she'd been staring, making him uncomfortable. Muttering an apology for her poor manners, she turned back to her dinner.

The rest of the meal concluded in silence, and without further mishap. All the while, however, Clara's mind considered her observations, wanting nothing more than to restore as much normalcy to her nephew's life as she could manage, if nothing else.

After all, occasional coarse behavior was not all she had picked up from her husband.

The next morning dawned on a miracle of transformation. For the household, anyway. Apparently, Farthingham had returned in the night after having secured both a new nanny and day servants to care for the manor. By the time Clara and Fritz came down to breakfast the lamps had been lit, the dust banished, and a full service laid out in the dining room.

Filling their plates from the sideboard, they sat down to table as Rockford entered the room. Her cousin nodded a greeting as he poured himself a cup of tea and took his place at the head of the table, unfolding his morning paper.

"No food?" Clara murmured, her tone neutral, though her gaze was not. "And where is Malcolm?"

More composed and less harried than the day before, Rockford lifted a brow and shook out his pages. "If you must know, *Mother*, I have already eaten. And Malcolm took his meal upstairs to better acquaint himself with Mr. Christopher Frost, his new caregiver and tutor."

Fritz smirked at her cousin's jibe—which she would take up with her husband later—but for the moment she ignored the ribbing, too caught up in delight.

"Oh! That is wonderful!"

A faint smile curved Rockford's lip. "I am so glad you approve. Now, I am afraid I must go to town shortly to attend business. Would the two of you care to join me? I must warn, I don't know how long I'll be."

Clara caught her inner lip between her teeth. How to politely decline?

Before she could formulate what to say, her husband lightly patted her knee out of sight beneath the table and cleared his throat. "Actually, I would. I must call on our solicitor, Jameson, and deal with a few matters that could not be resolved by correspondence. But Clara," and he turned her way with a gentle smile, "woke feeling a bit poorly this morning. Best she stays close to the manor, right, my love?"

As her cheeks faintly flushed, Clara ducked her head at her husband's implication. More to take up with him, surely, though his response was well suited to her preference. "By all means, darling. I had hoped to catch up with Malcolm and Mrs. Talliwight, after a bit of rest."

What better opportunity to observe Malcolm and work out how to improve his situation, by mechanical means or otherwise.

When would Clara learn to leave machinations to her husband?

Her intentions aside, Malcolm spent all day sequestered with his new tutor, who had shooed her from the room when she'd ventured above stairs to check on her nephew. Vexed, she'd gone to the kitchen looking for something to occupy her, only to come up hard against Mrs. Talliwight's territorial glower.

Regretting her decision to stay behind, Clara retreated to the library, but found little there to hold her attention. She had never been one for novels, and her collection of tomes on physics and mechanics and such had long ago been supplanted by Rockford's preference for philosophy, law, and business acumen. Though, one shelf held a number of books on music theory and performance that might bear examination. While Clara had a passable talent for the piano and the harpsichord, her skill and knowledge ended with a debutante's standard instruction in such.

Other than the occasional visit home, she had had little opportunity to play since leaving the manor, what with becoming a mother and their recent travels — even a cottage piano would be a bit much on an airship. A part of her missed the soothing practice, cocooned in tempo and rhythm and melody, the cascading notes enveloping her, transporting her. With her thoughts caught in the thrall of music, Clara moved to the salon, where her father had kept his prized Steinway, along with an assortment of other instruments. Surely, that would engage her for a while.

The door squealed as she pushed it open and the air inside felt stale, tickling a sneeze from Clara's nose. She frowned at finding the salon dark, the drapes drawn, presumably against the weather. By memory, she reached to her right to turn the knob on the wall beside the door — another of Fritz's ingenious modifications — both starting the flow of gas to the lamps and igniting it. The warm glow of the flames beneath their honeycombed mantles lit the room, revealing a sobering sight. While all was in place as she remembered, protective cloths covered everything in the room, whilst a thick layer of dust covered all of the cloths. Her heart ached at this further evidence of how drastically things had changed in the household.

Closing the door behind her with a click, she moved toward the enshrouded Steinway. How many hours had she spent at this bench practicing one composition after another until each met with her instructor's satisfaction? While she hadn't a passion for the vocation, she likewise hadn't loathed her lessons. In fact, she regarded them quite fondly.

Careful not to disturb the dust any more than necessary, she caught up the edges of the cover and folded them over, capturing the fine particles as much as possible. She then set the bundle aside and lifted the fallboard, revealing familiar, well-polished keys. Pulling out the cushioned bench, she settled herself, shoulders back, arms relaxed, fingers positioned just so, as she'd been taught. She then ran through her scales with the lightest of touches. Not bad. Not bad, just the slightest bit out of tune.

Both the instrument and *myself,* Clara thought, with a soft chuckle.

She drew a deep, steadying breath, closed her eyes, and began Mozart's *Sonata in C Major* from memory, one of the few pieces she could, it having always been her favorite.

Caught up in the music, she barely noticed the door squeal once more as she continued to play. Hearing rapid, staccato steps crossing the marble tiles, however, her eyes drifted open. She gasped at the unexpected sight of Malcolm lunging toward the piano, his expression a swirling maelstrom of longing and torment and rage. Her fingers forgot their placement, crashing down on the wrong keys. She jerked back just as he slammed down the fallboard, but not quickly enough.

Crying out, she clutched her left hand to her chest, the tips of her fingers throbbing.

Nothing but horror now upon his face, Malcolm whirled and ran from the room.

"Are you sure you're alright?" Rockford inquired, the worry and strain had returned full force to his demeanor once she finished explaining what happened.

"Yes, yes. Of course." Clara said, only by the most ruthless of efforts keeping her annoyance from her voice. She wished her cousin wouldn't hover. Fritz was bad enough.

As she sat on the settee in Rockford's study, her husband crowded her, holding chipped ice against her bruised fingers. Though he projected calm, she knew him well enough to note the faint tremors that coursed through his rigid frame. Fritz might hide it out of politeness, but he was furious. A state which served none of them well.

Withdrawing her hand from beneath his, she ran her fingers along his arm, willing her own annoyance away to soothe his. "I'm fine," she murmured, reaching up to draw his head down to hers until their gazes locked. Fritz blinked first. Then her husband drew her close, letting out a tremulous sigh.

Cradled against his chest, Clara asked, "Please, Fritz, could you go ask Mrs. Talliwight if I might have some tea?"

Though he didn't look happy about leaving her, Fritz did as she requested.

Once the door closed, Clara turned toward her cousin. "Rockford, what happened with the nanny? The caregiver before Mr. Frost?"

Rockford tensed, perhaps even flinched, but she did not spare him her gaze, pinning him beneath it until he responded. His head lowered until his chin nearly rested on his chest. For a moment, she thought he would not answer, but then he let out a quavering breath.

"This is my fault. I should have warned you. Malcolm…" He cleared his throat. "Malcolm came upon her playing his violin. He snatched it away and slammed it against the hearth, wrenching her wrist in the process. The poor woman was understandably traumatized and withdrew her service, recommending an asylum."

Clara closed her eyes, her heart aching for her nephew, and for her cousin. How could she have been so thoughtless? Why hadn't she realized how painful hearing music would be to Malcolm? No wonder. Her heart ached for him even more. Then what Rockford last said registered.

Drawing a sharp breath, Clara let out a soft *ohhh*.

She hesitated, but only a moment. "Rockford, she might be right."

Her cousin recoiled, jerking upright with more than a bit of heat in his gaze. "I beg your pardon?" he bit out between clenched teeth.

Clara raised her hand, gesturing for him to wait. "No, not an asylum, of course, but perhaps he would benefit from psychotherapy? After the loss he's experienced… He's closed so much up inside. Rockford, he looked positively tormented earlier."

For a long, tense moment, he considered her words.

"I will take your suggestion under advisement, cousin," he finally responded, his bearing and his tone both stiff and formal. Clara's good hand worried at her skirt, at a loss for how to make things better. She had come to help and accomplished only harm.

Just then, Fritz returned bearing a tray of tea and digestive biscuits. His step halted as he encountered the strained atmosphere of the room. Clara stood as he entered and for a moment, they all stared at one another in awkward silence.

"Well, I must admit, I could use some rest, cousin," Clara said, as she stepped toward Rockford and tugged him down to kiss his cheek. He let her, but he didn't ease the way. "I think it's best I take my tea upstairs and have a lie-down."

She turned and left the study, her husband trailing after.

Though resting had been a polite ruse to withdraw gracefully when she doubted her welcome, Clara woke to find herself curled atop their bed with her brooding husband watching her from one of the wing-backed chairs set before the fire.

Grimacing, she pushed herself up against the pillows and waggled her fingers at him. "All is well. I am fine."

Fritz nodded slowly, his intent gaze never leaving her.

"Truly," she said, dropping her hands to her lap.

"I know. But *he's* not."

Clara couldn't argue.

As the silence went on, though, and her husband's expression grew mulish, Clara sat forward, familiar with the outward signs of his inner conflict.

"What?"

Fritz scowled. "I don't know as I care to tell you now."

"Fritz…"

The scowl grew fiercer, with a hint of petulance.

Clara swung her feet to the ground. "What is it, Fritz?"

Instead of answering, he worried his lip until her patience wore out.

"Fritz, he is a twelve-year-old boy, you are an adult."

"He. Hurt. You."

She stood and went to her husband, sitting across his lap and wrapping him in her arms. Leaning into him, she murmured, "No. His hurt just splashed over on to me. He's in pain, so much pain, and all I want is a way to take that away from him."

Sighing, Fritz hugged her close. "Fine," he said, drawn out and reluctant. "I met with Charles and Sadie for lunch after my dealings with Jameson." Clara inhaled sharply at the missed opportunity to share a meal with her daughter and her dear friend, Charles Babbage. It had seemed the right choice at the time, but rather than help, she had only done harm by remaining at the manor.

Fritz continued, genuine excitement creeping into his voice, "Charles invited Sadie and me to a private salon, a performance by a group of musicians called the Divine Hand Ensemble. Clara, they might just be the answer to your prayers."

"How?"

Now he outright grinned. "You're gonna have to see."

Nothing could have prepared her for the Divine Hand Ensemble. Nothing.

The next afternoon, Fritz put on a dapper suit and helped Clara into a stylish frock, then they had Doyle fire up the boiler on the steam-carriage and drive them to town.

Anticipation had Clara once more at the edge of her seat as the countryside passed, fresh air and fields giving way to townhouses and other metropolitan establishments. For a time, she'd lowered the window to better view their progress, but as they reached more urban streets, her nostrils pinched with the… scents born of close habitation, faint though they were when traveling through gentrified areas, there was no avoiding the mingling of soot with the air, occasionally soured by a hint of sewage. Blowing sharply through her nose, she secured the window and settled back.

"We'll be there soon," Fritz said, drawing her to his side and pressing his lips to her hair.

"Might I know where *there* is?"

He smirked. "You'll see, shortly."

Clara hardly noticed as moments later they pulled to the curb in front of The Hanover Square Club, a private and prestigious establishment of some notoriety in London society. As they had approached, through the carriage window she spied two familiar figures waiting patiently before the building, one young and ebullient, the other of a respectable age and stoic. Clara's heart fluttered and her hand came down on her husband's arm, gripping tightly as a smile blossomed across her face.

Fritz laughed and drew her hand into his. "Careful, love. Best to not leave bruises."

"Sadie! And Charles!"

Her husband kissed her knuckles. "Of course, we could scarcely see one without the other, now, could we? Babbage has been a father long enough to know he's not to leave a young child unattended."

It had only been days since Clara had seen her daughter, but it felt much longer. Could it be possible Sadie had grown an inch? Surely not… She looked so pretty in her simple yoked dress, with her hair drawn back by a curious band, that when they drew closer, resembled a delicate clockwork butterfly that slowly fluttered its wings. Charles's work, surely.

For once, as Doyle lowered the step and opened the steam-carriage door, Clara did not wait for her husband to disembark and guide her down.

"Sadie!" Clara called out, her tone joyous, even as her daughter cried out, "Mama!"

As she and her daughter embraced, Fritz came up behind them, resting one hand on Clara's shoulder while extending his other in greeting to their old friend, Charles Babbage.

"You've cut it close," Babbage said by way of greeting, his brow dipping and his lips bowed in a frown, but the crinkles around his eyes spoke otherwise. "They've begun seating. The doors will close shortly."

Clara straightened, her arm around her child's shoulders. "My apologies, Charles. Shall we go in?"

The inventor *hmph*ed and gestured for the Langstroms to precede him, as if he expected they might wander off. Clara smiled, happy to see her gruff friend once more. They hadn't had long to visit when she and Fritz had delivered Sadie to his residence before departing for Chadsworth Manor. Such matters, however, faded into the background as she entered the edifice at Hanover Square, decades' past, one of London's premier musical venues. It had since been purchased by the Hanover Square Club, who reserved it for more exclusive purposes.

Tonight's appeared to be, in an echo of the past, some manner of orchestration. Per the clapboard staged in the lobby, a private performance by The Divine Hand Ensemble, featuring Mano Divina on Theremin. Clara frowned just the slightest, unfamiliar with the performer or the instrument.

"Fritz," she murmured back to her husband, "what is our purpose this evening?"

"You'll see."

She huffed at his secretiveness but forgot her annoyance as they entered the performance hall, impressed by the frescos on the arched ceiling high overhead and the plush seating, all but the first few rows cordoned off. Four seats stood open in the front row. Clara flushed and hurried her steps, chagrined to be the last to be seated, and so prominently.

"I am so sorry," she murmured.

Charles shushed her and waved her forward.

As they settled in their seats, the Ensemble began. Clara's hand pressed against her chest, her bruised fingers slightly aching, as the haunting notes of violin, cello, and bass wove point and counterpoint with one another, joined by sweet-sounding harps and… was that a vibraphone pacing the melody with its resounding beat? She had heard of the instrument, and briefly read passages about it just yesterday in the library, but this was the first she'd ever heard it played. Lovely, no doubt, but she could not fathom how this would possibly help Malcolm; to the contrary, in fact, such a performance would but reinforce his losses. She turned to Fritz, her perplexed gaze meeting his over their daughter's head. He merely smiled and nodded toward the performers, mouthing the word "wait."

Once more, she huffed. While delightful, nothing about the night's performance…

And then she heard it. Haunting, indeed, but more to the point, she saw. From the recesses of the curtain, a man sporting a dark, slightly silvered mane and resplendent in tux and tails wheeled out a peculiar contraption. Mano Divina, she presumed, and his… theremin, was it? Clara had never seen the like before. A box about a foot long and just a few inches high with nobs across the front. On one side a metal rod pointed toward the ceiling, and on the other a rod bent in a somewhat u-shape. He moved to the center of the stage where a table held what appeared to be a bank of Glassner batteries linked one to the other beside one of Thomas Edison's sound amplifiers. The performer connected his theremin to the waiting assembly by an insulated wire. The whole of it looked more like scientific equipment than musical instrument. But as she watched, the man took his place beside the theremin, and with the presence and showmanship of a conductor, began his orchestration, but with no baton, only movements of his hand, producing the most ethereal notes seemingly from the air itself, reaching into her soul and drawing her to the edge of her seat.

Clara gasped as the music ended to resounding applause, hers included. Her heart raced and her breath came in shallow pants. When she placed her hands to her cheeks, she found them flushed. Amazed, she turned to her husband as realization dawned.

This. This was the answer. Or so she fervently hoped.

After a few polite greetings and regretfully declined invitations, Clara and her family, along with Babbage, exited the club to find Doyle and the steam carriage waiting with the other conveyances of the more typical horse-drawn variety. He had drawn quite a crowd of gawkers. Not all of them looked best pleased about the new-fangled carriage, others just looked curious. Doyle was ignoring them, one and all, but promptly shooed them away as his employers approached.

"Evening, all," Doyle greeted them, as he moved to open the carriage door.

Returning the greeting, Clara turned to Babbage. "May we see you home?"

Before he could answer, Sadie Rae let out a squeal and clambered into the carriage, patting the seat beside her, her butterfly fascinator fluttering wildly. "Uncle Charles, you can sit next to me!"

With a sardonic quirk to his lips, Babbage tipped his head to Clara and motioned her into the carriage, before following. Fritz instructed Doyle of their destination, then climbed inside to take his place, tapping on the carriage top to signal the driver to proceed once they were all settled.

Clara longed to ask Charles about the Ensemble but was not sure how her questions would be received. Instead, Sadie Rae carried the conversation, her daughter going on in great detail of her last few days with Uncle Charles, very little of which Clara heard, with her mind awhirl with how they might better Malcolm's situation. But one comment did leap out at her.

"Wait... *you* made that?" she asked, sitting forward so abruptly, Fritz lunged to steady her, lest she bounce off the edge as the carriage ran over the cobbled street. Clara scarcely noticed as she paid greater attention to the delicate clockwork butterfly gracing her daughter's head.

"With Uncle Charles's help."

Babbage hmphed, as was his fashion. "I merely let you into my workshop, my girl. You are responsible for the rest."

Clara's hand went to her lips as awe filled her heart. *Already. So young and already so bright and clever.* Her thoughts went to Malcolm, sobering with much deeper understanding of his loss. She tucked that away rather than cast a shadow over the evening. Instead, with an exaggerated groan, she slumped back against her husband. "Two of them! I have *two* artificers to contend with."

Fritz chortled, raising his hands defensively as she swatted at him, even as a smile danced about her lips. Inside, her heart welled with pride to see her daughter already expressing such passion for "tinkering," as her husband called it. On that, they differed. Clara called it the genius of invention.

In any case, in short order, they arrived.

As Doyle opened the carriage door and lowered the step, Babbage descended to the street and guided Sadie down. He then turned and said, "Well, come on. You might as well have tea."

Being reasonably acquainted with Charles's kitchen, Clara went to ready the offered tea while the others settled in the parlor to chat. As she carried in the tray, her breath caught in her throat at the sight of them, Charles in his usual chair by the fire, Fritz beside him, with Sadie kneeling on the floor passionately going on in detail about something or other. A reminder of another time not long past, when Charles's former apprentice, Ali, had held the spot on the floor, imparting unexpected wisdom. Another bright and clever soul enthralled with invention.

And again, Clara's thoughts returned to Malcolm, his brilliance shadowed by pain, his music — for now — silenced. Setting the tray down on the table and pouring for each of them, Clara then perched on the edge of the divan and cleared her throat.

"Take a drink if your throat's dry," Charles groused. "That's what the tea is for."

Not the least put off by his brusque manner, Clara smiled and sipped at her cup, before asking, "Charles, the man that played today, Mano Divina, what do you know of him? Of his theremin?"

"Bah! Sensationalism! A fad! That's what I know of him. Airy engineered the invitation to taunt me with yet another example of 'invention taken *beyond* the theoretical.' Blast the man! He wouldn't know genius if one drew him a diagram."

Clara stiffened and resisted the urge to recoil, not expecting such vehemence, but then, she'd been unaware of George Airy's role in the evening's entertainment. That did pose a problem. Airy was Charles's bitter rival. She sat back with a sigh.

Her old friend shifted in his seat like a bantam settling his ruffled feathers, perhaps aware of Sadie's wide eyes and sudden silence. "Why do you ask?" he queried, his tone much subdued.

Drawing a steadying breath, Clara leaned forward, willing to beard even *this* dragon for her nephew. "Rockford's son, Malcolm… his injuries have robbed him of his ability to wield a violin and bow. Fritz and I thought that perhaps this theremin might serve as a way to restore to him the music his soul longs to perform."

With a faint frown, Babbage nodded and reached to pick up his tea, his gaze distant as he mulled over the problem. Giving a final nod, he looked up at her. "Your logic is sound. You find out if the lad is even willing while I see if I can work out the rest."

She started to rise to thank him, but Babbage waved her off.

"Drink your tea and go home. Sadie and I have much work to do in the morning."

Clara and Fritz rode to the manor in peaceable silence, with only the sound of gravel crunching beneath the wheels and the occasional hiss from the steam engine to interrupt their clamoring thoughts. It was all well and good to know a way Malcolm might regain his ability for music, but how to even broach the subject? Both Rockford and Malcolm were raw with this torment.

Finally, Fritz broke the silence.

"Do we even know if he'll be capable?" he asked. "I mean, the motions… Divina may not have wielded an instrument or bow, but his hands were in constant motion, contorting and shifting with precision to produce the various sounds."

Clara nodded, acknowledging she heard, but still wrestling with an answer.

"I *believe* so, but I cannot say for sure. At dinner the other night Malcolm's movements seemed controlled save when finer dexterity was called for, but to be certain, he must try."

Fritz frowned. "I can think of nothing so cruel than to offer hope only to have it dashed. What if the motions prove beyond him?"

For a moment, Clara could not breathe, every muscle in her chest frozen at the thought of the pain such failure would cause. That *she* would cause. She sat forward, gasping, and Fritz's hand came to rest on her back, gently rubbing until she remembered the art of breathing.

She filled her lungs and emptied them, and then again, each effort deeper than the last until they remembered their task.

"We have to try," she answered. "But first, we will test his mobility in the morning. And take a look at that brace while we are at it. I'm not at all sure it's serving any good."

Fritz nodded and tugged her back beside him against the cushions. "My clever girl. But no, *first* we speak to Rockford and make sure our efforts are welcome."

Clara frowned, more used to taking charge than asking permission. "Yes, of course."

And with that, she lay her head upon her husband's shoulder and let the rocking of the carriage lull her to sleep.

Having a plan was all well and good, but Clara found executing one much harder in practice. At least in their current circumstance. When they went down to breakfast the next morning, they discovered Rockford had gone to town, and Malcolm was already sequestered with his tutor.

She sat there picking at her crumpet while her tea grew cold, her mind searching for some path forward. Even once they secured Rockford's permission, they still had challenges to overcome. Operating this theremin required electricity, and while London's streets were lit by electric arc-lamps, her buildings relied on gas. Outside of town, only the mills and foundries availed themselves of such innovation.

"Fritz," she said, turning toward her husband.

"Oh, you've remembered I'm here."

Clara blushed and looked down at her tortured crumpet. "Sorry, only, I've been thinking."

He smiled and patted her hand. "You were saying?"

"How expensive is a battery arrangement such as they had on stage last night?"

Fritz's expression turned pensive; his gaze distant as he pondered.

"Well, I have been keeping up on Tesla's work on multi-phase generators. Fascinating how he employs the principles of alternating…"

"Fritz!"

"Sorry, love."

"You were saying?"

"I expect a generator would serve better. With the right materials and the use of Charles's workshop, I could build one sufficient to this need."

"What need would that be?" Rockford asked from the doorway, still wearing his coat, with his bowler in his hand.

Clara stood and took a step forward, for some reason feeling guilty. "Oh! Cousin, I thought you were off to town."

"I was. I forgot some important documents. Now, what need?"

She exchanged a glance with Fritz, who nodded, before she turned and moved to Rockford's side.

"We went to a marvelous performance last night, and we think…" She glanced back at her husband, suddenly unsure. The look of confidence he gave her eased her sudden fear. Clara turned back toward Rockford. Taking his hand, she drew him to the table where Fritz still sat. "We… Fritz and I believe we have found a way to give Malcolm back his ability to perform music."

Rockford frowned. "I beg your pardon?"

Before she could explain, a gasp sounded by the door, followed by rapid footsteps disappearing in the distance. Shortly thereafter, the manor door slammed.

Dusk had begun to darken the sky and they still had not found Malcolm.

As soon as they had realized what had happened, Rockford had rallied the servants and set them to searching the manor and the grounds, along with Clara and Fritz and even Mr. Frost, though he was likely to get lost himself. Not that it mattered. They scarce stood a chance against a lad reared on the property his entire life.

"Malcolm!" Clara called out as she wended her way through the wooded area before the manor. "Malcolm!" In the distance, others echoed her cries. Of course, part of her reasoned that all their calling served was to warn the boy they drew near. She let her voice fall silent and pondered where *she* might hide, were she so inclined. Stopping, she turned a circle, surveying the property not from the perspective of one searching, but one seeking to hide.

Her chest tightened as she saw it. As she recognized the bitter logic.

With soft, unhurried steps, Clara walked toward the wreckage of the carriage house. The bushes where once she had laid her bonnet to keep it safe from soot were gone. The *door* she had oft entered to assess Fritz's progress was gone. The charred timber framework, the stone walls. Those remained, along with blackened copper pipes and fragments of glass. Clara nearly gagged on the smell, not just of smoke and cinders, but chemicals and scorched metal and lost dreams.

And there, in the darkened shell of the burnt-out husk, over in the corner, the bitter essence of despair.

Unmindful of her day dress, Clara picked her way through the ruin and carefully lowered herself beside Malcolm, guided more by his sniffles than by sight. She said nothing. Did nothing. Merely sitting there in solidarity until her nephew spoke *his* needs.

"I don't want it back," he muttered. "I never want it back! The practice, the performing, the constant demand to be a perfect little man on display. Their eyes on me at every turn. The whispers and judgement and speculation. If I am never lit by the footlights again it will be too soon!"

Clara bit back a soft *oooh*.

"I used to love it. The music, the melody, the intricacies of composition. Now the very sound makes me sick, because all I can see is the crowds, gawking like I am some particularly well-trained animal performing tricks, half of them in awe, the other half waiting for me to fail.

"I no longer want to play; I want to *create*… as Uncle Fritz does. To improve the world." His voice cracked, then broke, a cross between a sob and a mocking laugh falling from his lips. "And now…" He smacked his hand against the soot-blackened wall, the brace thudding. "…now I can do neither, and it is all my own fault, *this* is all my own fault…"

Clara's eyes widened in sudden understanding and silent tears trickled down her cheeks. She longed to reach for him, but she had caused enough pain acting on what she *believed* he needed, that she remained still, waiting for him to decide.

Slowly, as his sobs ceased to strafe his throat, Malcolm curled against her side, his arms wrapping around her waist as he finally gave voice to his heartache, a young boy never quite allowed to be one, not familiar enough with hope to see his future still lay before him, and the power to shape it lay in his own hands, as impossible as that seemed. Clara folded herself around him and pressed a kiss to his head.

Soft, shapeless murmurs slipped past her lips as she comforted him.

Now was for the purging of heartache. Tomorrow, they could plan.

Author's Note - While the Theremin was invented in 1920 and patented in 1928, I have taken the liberty of moving that timetable forward for the purpose of this story, inspired by actual performances by Mano Divina and the Divine Hand Ensemble at the Dorian's Parlor Socials held in Philadelphia between 2011 and 2014. Of course, the story you have just finished ended up quite different than I'd envisioned, as tends to happen when characters have their own tale to tell.

Trouble on the Water

A Tale from the World of the Silver Moon

Twilight at sea. Strong winds lashed the passenger ship *Merrimoore*, as the crew scrambled to drop sails and lash down cargo before the approaching storm. Slowly the great ship turned, her prow defiantly facing the onrushing black clouds.

At the ship's railing, Cael Axton barely noted the storm. His gaze centered on three airships racing across the edge of the cloud banks. A sudden flash of lightning showed drab, unmarked gray airbags, then he lost them in the growing dark.

Cael Axton turned to his wife, Rishima Blaque, and felt his expression go tight and stiff. He made every effort to shroud his fears. He had brought them to this. All of them. His beloved wife, his son, the unsuspecting crew and fellow passengers.

A violent crash sounded, as if someone had shattered those clouds, releasing their contents all at once. Wind and rain and lightning's fire lashed the seas with new fury. The storm would be on them in minutes.

Rishima said, "We had best get inside, my love."

Cael glanced toward the airships. Lightning flickered, and he counted four of them this time. Were they tracking him? Not long ago, he would have thought the idea preposterous, but more than once over the last month, air pirates had tried to snatch him, and there had been several attempted burglaries at his laboratory.

How had they found him? And why were they after his invention?

Only his cousin, Stephe, knew the particulars of their journey and why. Cael swallowed hard; guilt churned his gut. They were like brothers, right down to their features. Stephe had acted as decoy while he and his family left the city. Cael sent a silent prayer toward the Silver Moon asking mercy and deliverance for Stephe—for them all.

The deck began to roll uncomfortably.

"Cael!" Rishima called out as she clung to the railing.

"Wait here," he told her.

Staggering a bit, he crossed to their cabin, entered, and ran to the chest lashed to the floorboards beneath the porthole. It held the sum of their belongings. He knelt and thrust the lid open. With no regard for anything within, he yanked out clothing and other personal items until he had cleared the chest. Then, drawing his fist back, he smashed through the false bottom. He ignored the pain, tugging at splintered wood until the treasure beneath lay exposed.

Behind him, he heard a gasp—Rishima.

Of course, she had followed him. He pivoted on his knees to find her in the doorway, staring at him.

"What are you doing?" she cried.

Cael forced himself to remain calm, stoic.

"We must be careful," he told her. He glanced at the berth where their young son slept. "Don't wake Roebling."

Turning, he reached into the trunk and drew out a sealed, wax-dipped leather pouch. Neither sea nor storm could hurt its contents. Then he rose and moved to his wife's side. He drew her up, kissed her—a light, fleeting brush of his lips that, despite its gentleness, slammed his soul—and then slung the pouch's strap around her neck. He slid it down the front of her bodice, reached beneath the hem, and tucked the pouch itself into the waistband of the pantalets she wore under her skirts. The pouch didn't show, but she looked again with child, if only just.

"You must do exactly as I say," he told her.

"What—?" Confusion and doubt creased her fine skin.

"Go to the main salon. Stay there, out of the way, both of you. If you hear sounds of trouble, hide. If anyone finds you, let none know that you have this. Let none know you are my wife, or that Roebling is my son. Do you understand?"

"Why?" she moaned, the words barely a whisper.

He drew her tight into his arms and lost control enough to bite off a single sob. "They will hurt you, my love, both of you, for something even I do not understand." He kissed the crown of her head and squeezed his eyes shut. "For your connection to me and that which you now hide beneath your dress, but if they are ignorant of what you mean to me… what I've entrusted to you… you might be safe."

He forced himself to release her.

Reaching up, he drew one of two stout leather cords from around his neck. With hands that trembled, he looped it around his wife's neck. "If the ship is lost—"

Rishima cried out at his words. The still-sleeping Roebling stirred.

"If the ship is lost," Cael repeated as he lifted their son and pressed him into her arms, "find a high place, then snap the flare, and keep it pointed toward the sky. I will see its light and come for you."

"Promise me," she demanded, her expression tight and fierce.

"I promise you, my love, an I am able…"

"*No!* You promise me, you *will* come for us."

He nodded. Then the deck beneath them pitched more violently than before. A loud *crack!* rent the silence between them as something heavy crashed against the outside of the cabin. Wood splintered, and the salt and damp trickled in. The whole ship shivered, shook, then gave an almost human groan.

From outside sounded cries of "We're breached!" and "Abandon ship!" The *Merrimoore* began to cant to one side as more shudders ran through the deck underfoot.

Rishma clutched Roebling close to her breast. The boy murmured and stirred in her arms.

"Quickly! To the lifeboats!" Cael cried. He took his wife's elbow and propelled them both before him. For now, pirates were less of a concern than the storm. If the ship went down…

They hurried aft toward the lifeboats following the other passengers. Rain lashed down. Waves sent geysers of spray over the sides of the ship. Roebling began to wail.

The crew helped the passengers into the lifeboats. "Women and children first!" the captain called. "Women and children to the front!"

Someone pulled Rishima forward. She and Roebling made it into the first lifeboat, along with a dozen others. Cael saw the pale oval of her face in a flash of lightning. Distantly, he heard her voice call out to him, but he could not make out the words.

Someone grabbed him from behind. He yanked his arm back and half turned.

Another flash of lightning revealed a dagger pointed at his gut. Then a hand reached out and yanked the flare from around his neck. And the grinning face—

"*Stephe…*" Cael breathed.

Drac Piltin braced himself against the flight console of his ship, *Talon*, his legs wide and his grip on the edge tight as he glared out the thick viewing glass at the remains of his other ships raining down upon the hungry ocean.

"Change course."

The men at the helm cringed at the snarl in his voice.

And well they should. Bad enough Axton had had time to flee, but now the inventor and his research were likely lost to the sea. The men who had allowed it would pay. Drac had not come to command his air pirate fleet by acting on assumptions, though. He narrowed his gaze.

"Mark the coordinates of that wreckage," he ordered the navigator, a finger jabbing toward where the waves swallowed the *Merrimoore*. "Then skirt the storm until this blow dies down and we can search for what we came for."

The men paled and their jaws clenched tight, but they did not say him nay.

Drac turned his gaze back to the fury of the storm and felt a force akin to it growing in his chest. Were these flares to find wide-spread use pirating would become a more perilous trade, with the risk of others coming to their victims aid cutting into profit. Thinking of the advantage these *flares* could afford his prey, he vowed he would control Axton and his prototype, preventing anyone else from making more.

Excepting himself, of course…

Rishima clung to the rocky outcrop with one hand, her other twined tightly around her son. Soon after they had reached the water the waves had capsized the lifeboat. All had been lost save themselves. She and her son had clung to a piece of the shattered boat until finally they drifted close to this haven. She'd tried to climb higher, even kicking off her skirts and soft-soled boots in an effort to gain better purchase on the rock, but beneath the water muck and slime coated the surface. The waves slammed into them in a constant barrage, grabbing their limbs and what remained of their clothes, trying to draw them back into the sea. It was all she could do to cling to both the outcrop and her son.

A sob broke free, then another until she could not help but wail as much in frustration as fear. When Roebling joined her in her cries, she drew him closer and clung to the rock, letting her tears fall. She had no energy to spare for remaining strong. She scrambled for a better hold on both rock and son, then huddled there. The mound of Cael's wax-coated pouch—still tucked firm in the band of her pantalets—mocked her from where her stomach pinned it against the outcrop. If she had even a spark of energy more her cries would have risen even higher. The leather cord around her neck, with its broken stub of glass, floated free before her like an accusation. Somewhere between the pitching deck and the sea the flare her husband had given her had shattered. She clenched her teeth on a keen, wondering if perhaps it would be best to just let go and let the sea draw them into its embrace. The next instant shame cramped her belly. How could she think such a thing? She renewed her efforts to scramble higher but failed to do more than remain somewhat steady as the sun turned its back on the day to slide beneath the horizon.

As darkness joined the ranks of her tormentors Rishima trembled in the grips of cold and wet and panic. Roebling's cries broke, then fade into fragmented whimpers. Numb, Rishima searched for words to reassure him, but they went unspoken as her son slid from her hold to disappear beneath the water.

"No!" she cried out, and immediately released her grip on the stone to dive after him. Panic lent her strength as she thrust her hands out before her and grabbed his coat just as the currents tried to suck him down. Jaw clenched and her expression drawn tight and fierce, she tugged him upward and kicked back to the surface. With the last of her adrenaline surge she managed to latch on to the rock and cling, too tired to even weep in silence.

Drawing her son close to her, she rested her forehead against the rough surface and bent all her will to holding fast. She had to believe that even without the aid of the flare Cael would find them. Her heart harbored no doubt. She held tight to that thought every bit as much as she clung to the rock.

Nearby something splashed into the water, the sound much different than the slapping of the waves. Rishima shivered and tried not to panic. She knew something of the manner of creatures that lived in the sea. And hunted there. Some were harmless, but not all. Soundlessly she prayed to the Unseen Moon for deliverance.

Peace settled over her spirit and she pressed a kiss to Roebling's brow, willing him to absorb the comfort and quiet his cries. He huddled closer and suddenly tensed. His cries rose in pitch and Rishima's calm vanished as something shoved him upward and out of her grip.

Before she could react, her son lay hard against the stones, staring back at her with eyes gone wide in a face that had never been so pale. His lip quivered, but he made no sound.

The next instant something pressed against Rishima's bottom, at once like fingers, but not. She shrieked as the unseen force pushed her out of the water as well. Her body slid across spray-soaked rock until she landed hard against her son. Grabbing him, she scrambled higher on the outcrop, holding him tight to her breast as she peered back toward the water.

Something peered back.

Eyes, black and unblinking, in a face both too human for comfort, and not enough so.

Rishima shrieked again and clutched her son closer, nearly fumbling her hold on the rock.

What tales she knew of the sea folk said they were a boon to sailors. That they aided those who made their living upon the sea. But what if the tales were not true? Rishma thought she saw something akin to remorse in that inhuman gaze. And then it reached out to her with determination clear on its expression.

Rishima glanced down, unable to imagine what she would see. Her heart wailed at the sight of a flare the mate to the one that had hung from her neck, of which there remained only a jagged nub. The sea folk stayed where it was, its hand steady as if it waited for her to claim the flare. Fear held Rishima back, but not for long; without that flare she and her son were lost. Before the creature could withdraw, Rishima scuttled forward and snatched the flare away, bringing it tight to her breast as she scrambled back to her son and drew him close as well.

For a moment the creature stayed there, watching them. It then turned its gaze to the heavens briefly, with longing clear on its face, before diving again beneath the waves. When it was gone the tension drained from Rishima's body. For now, they were secure. The Unseen Moon had delivered them, though by means she never would have fathomed. She allowed herself a brief rest before attempting to string Cael's flare on the cord she took from around her neck.

Her hands trembled and the knot fought her but, determined, she managed, all the while telling herself that the return of the flare meant nothing dire. Surely the creature merely found it… Cael promised… *promised* to find them; that the flare would lead him to them. She'd never truly understood how, but she believed in him. He would come for them. He had to come for them!

But… what if he couldn't?

Rishma's shudders increased as she buried that traitorous thought and wedged herself and Roebie into the shelter of a nearby crevice as the waves picked up once more and rain pelted them from the sky. Pressed between them, strap snugged tight over her chest, Cael's pouch gouged her ribs. The desire to reach for her neck and ensure the flare remained secure flooded her mind, but her hands were occupied at the moment, desperately occupied. A deep, cold ache deadened her fingers, but she renewed her grip and muttered formless sounds of comfort in Roebie's ear. What she would not give to hear the same sounds from Cael's lips, and his body pressed tight against her back. Her hope flaked away like ash and her eyes closed in pain. The reminder was too much. Rishma threw back her head and screamed her husband's name. She had to believe, but her heart broke anew, knowing he may never come. The conflict tore at her soul as harshly as the wind and waves snatched at their bodies.

Scowling, she dragged her courage up and shoved the dark thoughts deep yet again.

All she had to do was hang on through this most recent storm. Once the sea had calmed and the sky cleared, she would do as her husband bid her. She would climb to the top of the outcrop, if need be, and snap that flare. Then Cael *would* come, and they would all be safe.

Tucking her son more firmly into the curve of her body, Rishma cleaved to the rock with both hands, clutching until her fingers bled while the heavens raged around her, and her heart within.

Argent Pulan—the senior member of the Order of the Light of the Moon—carefully climbed the still swaying guard walks to the Reflectory. The thin, switch-like upper branches of the silver oaks had been woven into a lattice of arches interspersed with meditation alcoves, all open to the sky and the rays of the Unseen Moon, to which their Order was dedicated.

He turned his gaze downward to scan the temple in uneasy silence. Something about these storms was not natural. They went counter to the influence of the moons. He could not fathom how that was possible. The moons controlled the tide, which fed the clouds. And yet Pulan saw signs of the disruption everywhere he looked as the clouds flowed back to their normal paths. And he was powerless to explain. Nature had yet to settle from the shake-up. In the branches, the creatures of the silver oak chittered and barked in agitation. There were faint creaks as those sleeping fussed in their slings.

Pulan paced and continued to watch the skies.

As leader, he was charged with the safety of this Order. At the moment there were many occurrences making him feel the weight of that responsibility: dense smoke in the sky off to the North where there should be none. Strange sounds and violent, unexplainable lights off in the distance in the dark hour, when there was no moon. An increased amount of men and wreckage washing up on the coast. Even now several battered survivors of the last storm rested in the infirmary. On or two would not likely see another moonrise.

Very little good took place in the dark hour.

Pulan's left hand fisted on a nearby vine, making it creak.

For some time now he had experienced a spirit of unrest, as if something predatory lurked in the surrounding clouds. In his right hand he held a brass spyglass, a gift from Captain Tyson, a merchant with whom the temple had long traded. The glass proved unhelpful, with nothing suspicious visible on the waters or the skies, despite the feeling that tightened every muscle Pulan had.

Thhurr... A soft, fluff-furred head pressed him just above his knee, distracting him from his dark thoughts. Pulan looked down into the sweet, flat face of Jaci, one of the temple's complement of tree cats. She'd balanced carefully on her back legs, bringing her head within petting distance of his hand. Pulan chuckled and collapsed the spyglass, sliding it into its belt pouch.

He leaned down and scooped up the cat, careful of the dewclaw, which contained a paralyzing neurotoxin useful to the tree cats when hunting vipers and other deadly creatures of the high silver oaks. She arched, then wrapped her four limbs around his arm with a pleased chirp.

It soothed him to run his fingers through her long, thick coat, to watch the shifting patterns of golden fur and deep brown markings frosted with silver, to feel the rumble of her purr against his chest. Indulging in the moment, he moved into a nearby alcove, a nest of woven branches and linen cushions with an arched opening sufficient to allow him to continue viewing the skies. From where he and Jaci sat, Pulan looked down upon the rounded edge of the temple's airship, *Mahnaz,* tethered hard and fast to the platform below, having docked before the first of last night's storms. They had just come off their circuit and were settled into a rest period…

Without warning, the tree cat in his arms growled, then seemed to triple in size, her fur puffing out. Pulan watched, fascinated, as instinct took the cat. Her ears swiveled and her head moved from side to side as if triangulating. Her jaw dropped open and her breath came in pants, drawing air across the scent glands in the roof of her mouth. Pulan lowered the cat to the plank flooring as she began to strain against his arms. Rather than race away Jaci wove in agitated circles around his legs, bumping against him insistently. Pulan frowned at the unusual behavior.

Growling again, she leapt to the base of the arch. Without another sound Jaci launched herself into the air, using air pockets in her puffed fur to surf the winds with the same ease that her northern cousins, the Lunam, used them to swim the waters below. The cat glided down to the platform. When she landed, she glanced up at him reproachfully and yowled before loping down the guard walk that lead to the infirmary.

As she disappeared beneath the canopy, Pulan finally heard the faint commotion that first caught her ear. Foregoing the long climb down through the network of interconnected walkways, he hefted himself up into the arch. The outside of the temple wore a loose skin of netting. He gripped it firmly and swung himself out, swiftly scurrying down the knotted length to the infirmary level. Increased sounds of disturbance rose around him the lower he descended.

He leapt the last few feet and ran toward the fracas.

Chaos shattered the normal calm of the infirmary. One of the storm victims lay unconscious on the floor. Another had been restrained across the bower. Fresh blood, bright crimson against cloud-white cotton, marred the bandage wound around his abdomen. Pulan could not say if it came from the wound beneath or from the new slash across the man's shoulder, near to the neck. Between the injuries and the haunted look in the man's eye, he looked like he had come off a battlefield, not been fished from the sea.

"Enough!" Pulan said, dropping his voice deep and keeping it low. That one word smothered all other commotion in the room, as healers and patients alike fell silent and turned their gazes to him. For a moment, nothing, then a rumbling *thurrr* nearly broke Pulan's stern countenance as Jaci circled his legs, bumping him before she strolled over to the patient still being held back. Astonishingly, the tree cat settled at the man's feet, leaning her frame against him as she continued to purr.

Pulan sighed and ran his hand over his face, pressing his fingertips firm against his temples.

"Please, explain," he requested turning to look at Argent Candra, the Order's senior healer. Her platinum hair lay smooth over a rumpled robe and a streak of blood marred her cheek.

"The man on the floor attacked this one," she answered, gesturing to the patient still standing. "I cannot say why, but we were trying to break things up when the attacker snatched a knife from one of the guards and… " She looked uncomfortable continuing, her face pale and her throat swallowing convulsively. Pulan held up his hand.

"Thank you. And how have we reached this state of affairs?" He gestured to attacker.

"Jaci," Candra said, nodding toward the cat.

Pulan gasped at that unexpected response. His gaze went from what he now knew to be a corpse on the floor, to where the tree cat still leaned. She stared serenely back. Blinked. Then lifted her front leg and casually, but intently began to clean blood from her dewclaw.

"Well… that explains that one. And the other?"

"Before he succumbed to the toxin, the attacker said something… 'they are lost to you.'"

"What does that mean?"

Candra frowned, compassion glittering in her gaze. "I don't know, but the other was quite distraught. He is held to keep him from leaving, not from attacking."

Before they could continue, the man's legs buckled. This time controlled chaos reigned as the medical staff returned him to his bed and gave him care, while the guards dealt with the body.

In the light of day, without the wind plucking at them or the waves slamming them against the rocks, Rishima sprawled in the shade of the stone spire, Roebling curled beneath her arm. Dried salt stiffened her soft cotton pantalets and cracked her skin. Moving was agony, between the sting of the salt and the ache of her bones and bruises. She lay as still as she could manage beside her sleeping son. If only she could join him in that blessed state, but each time she closed her eyes she saw a host of dreadful images: black, alien eyes; a scaled hand reaching for her; Cael floating beneath the water, his eyes empty… Rishima shuddered as she searched the waves and the skies for any sign that Fate might show them mercy. She spied a dark speck among the clouds too large for a bird on the wing. An airship, then. More pirates? A courier? For want of that answer, she could not move, could not clamber up to where it would do some good to break the flare and release its beam of light.

Rishima wept silently and curled her body around Roebling. They could not stay here, yet she was afraid to use the flare. Afraid of whom it might summon, if anyone at all. Afraid she would use it too soon, or too late, and have it spent and wasted. Were it not for her child she would not mourn a death upon these rocks, for it was harder and harder to tell herself that Cael searched for them, but Roebie did not deserve such an end.

Rishima levered herself up, disengaging from her son, her skin screaming as it tore further, letting in the crumbs of salt. It took grim determination, but she scaled higher on the outcrop, as high as she could go and still have a hope of climbing back down, and then she stopped. Perched on a narrow ledge of rock butted up against the tallest spire, she stared out at the endless sea. Other than a thin ribbon of green on the horizon to her left, nothing but water and sky greeted her eyes. Even the airships she had spied earlier had vanished. Rishima wanted to weep but found she could not, though her eyes ached with the need.

How long would the flare last? Cael hadn't told her. What if it was short lived? Was there any point in breaking it now, when there was no vessel in sight to see it? Uncertainty paralyzed her, left her clinging to her perch doing nothing for long enough that the sun baked her further as it rose up over the spire.

"Momma?" her son's tremulous cry rose from below. "Momma, where are you?"

Rishima found she could not answer; her throat too dry to give voice to words.

"Momma? I am so hungry… so thirsty… Momma?" The fear and suffering in her son's voice decided her. Were she to wait much longer there would be no point. Gently drawing the cord from around her neck, Rishima looked around. There was a weathered crack in the spire, leaving a carbuncle of rock clinging to the side. If she wrapped the cord firm around the protrusion and wedged the flare down into the crack, the beam would remain pointed to the sky without her hand to hold it, the rock itself offering some protection from any weather.

Breathing deep and lifting continual prayers to the Moon, Rishima gently tapped the top of the flare where the glass was scored, as Cael had shown her, until it cracked, then a little harder to break the cap away. She fumbled as the compound frothed to fill the glass tube and the chemicals reacted to the air with a bright flash that dazzled her eyes and left her disoriented. The bitter fumes sent her into a coughing fit. Instinctively she grabbed the rock to steady herself and almost lost the precious flare. Sobbing, she tightened her grip. Before aught else could happen she quickly wound the cord and snugged it tight, leaving the open flare bound flush to the rock face, a deep, green light lancing from its base far up into the sky.

Cael woke to a small, soft body curled against his. He smiled and reached out, expecting tousled hair and his young son's slender limbs. A tortured groan cracked past his lips as he encountered fluffed fur and the rasp of a rough tongue across the back of his hand. Sleep's fog lifted, leaving only heartache and a dull pain, which he felt the length of his body. He opened his eyes to a view of the twilight sky framed by a woven arch.

Slowly he blinked. Then blinked again, hesitating to believe the evidence of his eyes. *My fare... It has to be my flare,* he thought, as in the distance vibrant green lit a swath of sky like a beam of sunlight shone through an emerald lens.

In silence, he both laughed and cried.

Cael glanced around. Other patients slept in their cots, but for the moment there were no attendants in the room. The cat did not protest when he set it aside and slid from his bed. It did not protest as he pulled on his clothing. It yowled the moment he tried to sneak through the door arch closest to where he spied his flare's beacon. Though Cael tried to ignore the beast, his shoulders tensed as he left the bower, only to discover the way only lead to an alcove, one currently occupied by a woman with pale gold hair. He had a vague recollection of her *tsk*ing over him before as she stitched his shoulder.

"Good morning," she said, as if finding nothing amiss about him creeping around in the early hours.

He nodded but said nothing as he slowly backed into the main bower. The woman did not move from her seat but something soft did bump insistently against Cael's calf. He flinched and glanced down, half-heartedly cursing the cat that eyed him. When Cael looked up again he found himself face to face with the woman. This time he yipped and stumbled back. Flushing in embarrassment, he spun away and headed for a different arch.

Words softly spoken halted his steps.

"What is so important you would risk your health… your life?"

Cael pivoted to face her, his gaze unwavering, every muscle taut. "My family."

She watched him with soul-searching eyes the color of a spring sky. With an abrupt nod she looked past him. Cael spun, expecting the need to evade, but all he spied was a retreating back.

"What have you done?"

"No worries," she murmured as she slid past him to a ceramic carafe suspended above a small power stone. Steam wafted from beneath the lid as she lifted it off and poured the contents into a waiting mug. "You will drink this and then allow me to check your wounds. When I am done, you and I will have a conversation with Argent Pulan."

Cael glowered at her, his teeth gritting at her reasonable and un-yielding tone. He did not know this Argent Pulan and did not care what he had to say. All his thoughts were centered on finding a way to where the flare's light pointed. "And if I refuse?"

"The attendants come back, you drink the tea anyway, before returning to your bed, and we try again when morning has properly arrived." She then took a drink from the cup before offering it to him with a good-natured grin.

"As if that means anything," he grumbled as he drained the cup to the dregs, barely noticing the peppery taste of good bergamot tea, lightly sweetened. Next, she handed him the biscuit he had not noticed waiting beside the saucer. His stomach rumbled and twisted at the prospect. The woman laughed as he grabbed the treat before she could take her taster's bite.

"I am Argent Candra, the senior healer," she said, as she laid her hand lightly on his arm and guided him back to the alcove, gathering what looked like a medical kit from a cabinet as they passed. "We'll check you over in here, so as to not disturb the others." Cael glanced toward the row of cots, blankets mounded by sleeping patients. He nodded and followed her through the arch though he could not help but frown at the delay.

Crumbs trailed behind him.

He waited as she lowered a curtain over the opening and uncovered a vibrant power stone that lit the space as bright as day. The examination went swiftly and well, if the woman's soft murmurs were any indication. As she rewrapped Cael injuries a man cleared his throat from the doorway.

"Well, your prognosis?" the stranger asked.

"I believe Jaci's been helping him along," she said. "He looks two weeks' healed instead of just two days."

As Cael pulled his shirt back into place he noted her respectful attitude and presumed this was Argent Pulan. Without waiting for niceties, Cael pivoted and moved to stand before the new arrival. "I need to go, sir, now."

"Go where?"

Cael moved to a nearby arch on the same facing as the one he'd seen upon waking. Pulling aside the drape, he pointed toward the beacon light. "Where that leads..." He felt Argent Pulan tense and awe tinged Argent Candra's indrawn breath.

"What is it?" she asked, coming closer.

"It is a power-stone flare," he told her, "an invention of mine, and I pray it leads me to my wife and son..."

... and not the traitorous Stephe, his thoughts snarled.

As Cael shoved that worry to the back of his mind, he quickly told his tale. The man called Pulan moved before the arch and lifted a spyglass to his eye. Cael watched as the Argent turned his head from one edge of the horizon to the other before coming back to the direction of the beam of light. "*Blessed Moon!*" Pulan said. "There is someone on the rocks."

Cael reached for the glass, waiting impatiently as the man showed him how to adjust the lenses for distance. He fought to still his hand's trembling as he brought the glass to his eye and turned the rings until the image came clear. The glass brought into focus a form that might well be his wife, though the distance was too far to tell for sure. Yet who else would know how to use the flare? He had not explained it to his cousin. Cael continued to scan the rock. He swayed where he stood.

My son, where is my son?

"Don't worry, young man," Pulan spoke from behind him. "It appears an airship is already investigating the light. Your loved ones will soon be rescued."

At the man's words Cael stiffened, the biscuit he'd eaten earlier suddenly like ground glass in his belly. He raked the spyglass across the skies in search of the airship mentioned. The spyglass would have been lost, if not for Pulan's swift reflexes. On seeing the familiar outline of the airship and the lack of any markings on the grey airbag, Cael dropped the instrument and spun away from the arch, crossing the alcove in two long strides and making it halfway across the main bower before he heard the other scramble to follow.

"What? What is it?" Argent Candra called after him, her voice no longer lowered out of consideration for those sleeping.

"That airship is piloted by the pirates who attacked our vessel."

Drac cursed as the helmsman bobbed the controls of the airship. Ahead—seemingly rising from the depths of the sea itself—a vibrant stream of green light shot toward the sky. His eyes narrowed as he realized this had to be the work of one of those cursed flares. He could just imagine the loot they would cost him if every ship had a ready means of summoning help. Time to make sure that innovation never became widespread.

Snarling, he smacked the helmsman across the back of the head as the 'ship continued to list.

"Get it together and head for that light... or we'll learn if you can safely hit the water when dropped hundreds of feet through the air."

Rishima knew true despair as the seas grew rough once again and clouds threatened to storm. Finding it difficult to hold both herself and her son to the slick rocks she wedged Roebling into the crevice they had earlier shared, knowing, should she falter, he would be more secure in there alone. She clung to the pillar beside him, her eyes locked on her beacon, praying for all she was worth the Moon would have mercy.

"Momma… " her son cried. "Momma, I'm frightened. I want to go home. When is Da coming to take us home?"

Her heart shattered. *Never*, it whispered. Aloud she spoke gently, "Shh… my boy, hold tight and all will be well. You must hold tight for Momma, do you promise?"

As the waves crashed about her legs and tugged on her, she could not tell if he answered.

Rishima searched the skies, tasting blood as her teeth worried her salt-cracked lips. She found it difficult to tell if the specks in the sky were shifting clouds or airships that meant their rescue… or ruin. She feared the return of the pirates that had sunk the *Merrimoore*, but she told herself she might at this point welcome even them, if only they would rescue her son. But deep in her heart she knew it would go ill for both of them should the pirates come to the beacon's call.

Continuous prayer slipped from her lips as another wave reared up and slammed her with all its fury.

Somehow Argent Pulan ended up on the wooden walkway in front of Cael. He dropped from above like a monkey until the boards swayed and Cael was forced to stop and grab hold of the guide rope.

"Where can you possibly think you are going when you know nothing of our temple?"

Heat flooded Cael's face and he ground his teeth on a growl, but could say nothing. He was, indeed, behaving foolishly.

The religious leader stared at him with a knowing, compassionate gaze before pointing the way Cael had come. "This is the wrong path… if we hope to get the airship launched before the pirates reach the rocks."

Cael felt tears sting his eyes as he turned to the side and let Argent Pulan pass. The walkway continued to sway as they hurried halfway back to the bower Cael had fled before taking an off-shoot that led outward to the treeline. There they paused at the edge of an open plank platform. At the far end an airship christened *Mahnaz* bobbed in the breeze on its' tether lines like a magnificent whale sunning itself on the surface of the sea. The wooden hull was smooth and well-finished in a dark, rich shade, a symbol of one moon against another moon artfully carved into the surface. The airbag floated above it, bound by a netting of cords to secure the balloon to the hull. Cael knew this was small for an airship, only a Stratus-class, but he felt dwarfed.

Halfway down the platform, just before the fixed wings, the cat waited beneath a braided cord that dangled down the side of the air-ship's ironwood hull. She looked as if she contemplated leaping up to yank the cord herself. Before she could prove him right or wrong, Argent Pulan gripped the cord, giving it one long pull and then two short. Within the vessel bells rang, followed by several solid thuds and faint cursing. Above, a narrow hatch the size of a man's head *thunked* open.

"May I help you, Argent Pulan?" he asked respectfully, though his expression appeared a bit disgruntled beneath his dark, sleep-rumpled hair.

"I must talk to Captain Migina, now."

The crewman looked doubtful, anxious, even, and certainly no longer a bit sleepy.

"Um... you sure about that?"

"I'm afraid so, Airman Torbin. I'm afraid so. It is rather urgent."

Cael's hands fisted at his sides and tension ran through his body like a stream of energy from a power stone. He wanted to scream at them to hurry, but restrained himself. The welfare of his family depended on their good will. Still, from his right, the green glow taunted him, as did the sinister dot making its way across the darkening sky.

Torbin let out a sigh. "If you'll wait here, I'll beard the tiger."

The Argent laughed as the crewman withdrew and closed the hatch. Cael chaffed at their seeming lack of urgency. Lest his tension get the better of his discretion and his tongue, he moved away to the edge of the platform, staring out over the sea. His gaze locked on the beacon that rose from that far outcrop. His brow furrowed and the muscles across his shoulders tensed further as the wind picked up and grey smudges marred the horizon. Even now he heard the *Mahnaz* strain slightly against its tethers, bouncing as cross-breezes dipped in from the opposite direction. He glanced down at the boughs beneath him.

The oak leaves turned up their bellies.

Behind him the hull creaked. Cael turned to spy the airship swaying with more vigor. Smaller branches rattled below. He frowned and returned to Pulan's side as the muffled sound of wood scraping against wood came from above. A larger segment of the hull sunk in and slid to the side. A tousled head of auburn hair poked through as a plank ladder dropped into the proper anchor points on the platform. It took an effort for Cael to restrain himself from hurrying toward that ladder. Instead he waited impatiently for the Argent to ascend first before gripping the rope supports and scrambling upward.

"What bother are ye about now," the woman groused, her brown eyes darkened and a bit sullen.

"Captain Migina, please rouse your crew, there is need of rescue out at sea, and I fear we will soon race the weather in addition to the pirates already underway."

Cael tried to stand out of the way as the captain grumbled and reached to close the hatch. Before she could swing it shut Argent Candra called out from below.

"Wait! One more coming up..."

She scampered up with more grace than Cael had managed, and that with a sack of medical supplies on her back.

"Good," Pulan said as he moved past the two women. "We may need you." Cael trembled at those words as he followed the Argent forward toward the command deck.

The sound of engines overhead woke Rishima from a weary stupor. Her head fell back more than lifted. Though her eyes blurred her vision remained clear enough to realize that the man descending the rope was not her husband. She blinked furiously and turned her gaze to the airship hovering above, shadowing the outcrop like a great dark cloud. The shape... the color. They were all too familiar. She'd last seen similar from the deck of the *Merrimoore* as airships much like this one bore down on them in attack.

She looked down at where her son slept, tucked in his crevice. He appeared nothing more than another dark mound of rock, curled as he was beneath his coat. No one would see him there. Praying he remained asleep, she set her jaw against the pain and forced herself upright while the stranger remained many feet in the air. With his focus on descending, she thought perhaps he had not yet seen her. Quietly and carefully, she crept around the base of the spire where she sheltered. Moving to where she knew she was out of sight, she scaled the rock once more, painful inch by painful inch, until she lay against the rock face, burning toes wedged in a narrow split just below where she had secured the flare. Only her slight size allowed her to perch without falling. She hugged the rough surface and prayed both she and her son went unobserved. From her vantage point, she took a moment to scan the sea and air as she had been unable to below. The waters thrashed in choppy waves undisturbed by any ship's hull. She peered further, toward the horizon, daring to lift a hand to shield her eyes, but to no effect. Not a sail to be seen, not even in the distance.

She turned her gaze in the other direction and nearly lost her grip on the rock. Another airship closed fast from the distant shore. The design and clear markings on its hull distinguished it from the pirate vessel overhead. She raised one arm and tried to wave, to give some sign of her presence. She saw no indication they had seen her.

As she drew her arm back, she felt a breath of air against her neck. Rishima tensed at the sensation, warm even for these climes. Her nose pinched at a foul odor wafting on that breeze. And then she heard a creak, as of a rope twisting. She screamed and flinched away as someone grabbed for her. The world spun and she was sure she would fall. Did fall, if only a moment.

A crude chuckle sounded above her as a thick, callused hand caught her by the back of her bodice. She looked up and glared at another pirate dangling from a second rope just above her perch. He already had what was left of the flare capped with a cork and tucked in a pouch at his waist. Even from there the glow of it cast a ghastly light over his rough, scarred features.

"Boo!" he said, breaking into loud, brash laughter as she flinched away from his foul breath.

As her gaze met his she knew her fate, should he succeed in drawing her up into that cursed ship. She dropped her eyes again and shuddered, but as the man continued to laugh she noticed his folly. Here he hung, one hand holding the rope, and the other her clothing.

From below she heard the faint cry of her son, startled awake by her cry. And there, near even with her chin, was the man's dagger. Her heart pounded and ached at the intention she considered. *Blessed Moon!* But could she do such a thing?

Could she reach out and grab that blade and thrust it through that shriveled heart?

Surely it would spell her death as well. Squeezing her eyes tight she could hear the approaching engines of the other airship, but scarcely believed they were close enough to do her a bit of good. But… her son… they would arrive in plenty of time to rescue Roebling. Really, truly that is all that concerned her, not her own life or the state of her soul. Cael had gone before her and she was not averse to following, if it meant her son would be safe and the pirates foiled for all time as the sea claimed the prize she hid.

Before she or the pirate realized it, her cracked hand closed on the well-worn hilt. She drew the blade and thrust it up beneath his ribs, then yanked it out with a twist. Her other hand grabbed the remains of the flare as the pirate's grip convulsively tightened at her back. Then, with a strangled gurgle, he tumbled from the rope, drawing Rishima with him.

His body slammed into the edge of the rocks, hers the water, but even so she knew no more as the waves closed over her head.

On the command deck of the *Mahnaz* Cael cried out and nearly dropped the spyglass again as he spied through its lens his wife caught up by a pirate dangling from the belly of the other airship. They were within yards of the outcrop but too far for him to intervene.

"Get me there, now!" he demanded, with no thought for decency or courtesy, only for his wife. He thrust the spyglass into Pulan's hands then dashed down the companion way toward the hatch. The captain must have used the call box to notify Torbin, because he stood there with the plank ladder ready to drop. Cael's throat tightened as he moved to the opening. When he glanced out they had drawn close enough for him to see the bleak determination shadowing Rishima's gaze. He watched as she lashed out. He screamed as she fell, even as pride welled in his chest.

Ignoring the ladder, Cael dove for the water where his wife sank. As he cleaved the sky he heard the sound of the airship's guns firing, warning the air pirates away. And then he broke the water cutting through the waves like a dart. Desperately he swam, his eyes open and searching. His lungs burned the closer he came to the rocks but fear kept him were he was, looking for his beloved. A stream of bubbles ripped the water around him drawing his gaze down. He nearly gasped at the sight that greeted him. All-black eyes stared up from a scaled face that somehow appeared startled, then awe-filled. The creature bowed its head in what seemed like reverence. The sight so confused Cael that he almost did not noticed the burden the sea folk held out to him.

Rishima!

Cael reached for her and tried to surge to the surface only to find his kicks lacked sufficient power. Dark spots drifted across his vision and he felt himself begin to sink. He struggled upward again determined to save his love but he had been under too long. Suddenly finned arms wrapped about his waist. Cael gasped and would have fought, but there was no time. With a powerful swish of its tail, the creature propelled them upward. Cael lost the breath in his lungs, but did not struggle as the water above his head lightened and then broke.

He gasped as hands reached down from above to haul him up and Rishima with him. As the *Mahnaz's* crew drew him and his wife onto the rocks, Cael's gaze locked with that of the sea folk, who watched him from just below the water's surface. Though he could not explain it, Cael had the sense some debt had been repaid.

Cael rocked back as Roebling flung himself around his neck. His son's small body filled his vision and gratitude to the sea folk welled within him. When he looked back the creature had disappeared beneath the waves.

Murmuring a quiet 'thank you,' Cael Axton clutched his family to his chest and watched as the pirates' airship fled across the sky.

As Rishima stirred against him, coughing and sputtering, he could feel the pouch press against him. Silently he cursed the thing and realized he would not care had it been lost, as long as his wife rest safe in his arms.

She looked up at him with dazed eyes and murmured… "You promised."

"Promise kept," he said as he gently, reverently pressed his lips to hers.

Angel de la Muerte

Aleta Angelina Fabricio knelt before her family's graves for a very long time.

Long enough, the end of one day became the beginning of the next. Long enough, the murmurs of the surrounding Día de los Muertos celebrations faded away as families went home or lay down to rest beside their loved ones' graves. Long enough, the autumn night's chill seeped through her cotton robe and into her bones. Lina nearly tumbled away at the barest touch on her shoulder, calling her back to the dark blanket of night and the low, smoldering embers of nearly spent candles glinting throughout the graveyard like fireflies. She would have fallen if not for the thick, sturdy haft bracing her. Her grip tightened on the smooth wood handle of Santa Muerte's scythe, which had replaced the cobbled-together prop Lina had left home with.

Slowly, as if fighting to turn against thick, clinging aether, Lina glanced up over her shoulder. Her right eye burned where the thin glass lens attached to her father's spirit goggles hugged its surface. The left merely burned from spent tears, as it bore no lens. She blinked and swayed, disoriented as the fading wisps of lingering spirits wafted in plain sight, though her goggles shouldn't function without being paired with those worn by her father's crow, Beltran.

Lina bit back a sob. She had lost both father and crow in one brief slash by her own hand, their spirits freed from an unfettered evil that had possessed them.

Shuttering that fresh pain, she focused on the moment, looking up at the one standing over her, nearly too far away to touch. Lina blinked and pushed the goggles to the top of her head, removing the glass disk from her eye so she could better see.

Much in the way of the restless spirits, the gaze she met swirled with intense emotion, in this instance, a mix of anger and hurt and concern. For a moment, reality seemed to flux between the spirit and mortal realm as if Lina's prolonged use of the goggles had caused the two to overlap. Wisps of aether clung to her grandmother's features, but Lina blinked, and they faded away. Even so, something seemed off with Abuela's color.

"Abuela…"

Her grandmother frowned down at her. Then she took in the goggles perched on Lina's head, paired with the calaveras mask and faded blue cotton robe she wore in a silent plea to Santa Muerte for her blessing, and the frown deepened. Lina and her grandmother had fought earlier over her manner of dress, and Abuela's disapproval clearly had not softened. The frown turned into a scowl, and Abuela quickly shuffled away to fuss over the oferenda, though she herself had arranged the altar earlier in the day.

"You plan to stay up all night, niña?"

Niña, not mija. The surface of Lina's heart cracked like aged porcelain.

She pushed to her feet. The hand she reached out to her grandmother trembled faintly as guilt pinched her belly. Her mother's mother shrugged away before they could touch. Lina frowned as a small ache settled in her chest. Her grandmother was all she had left, yet the two of them only seemed to spark like flint to steel.

Bad enough, they had fought on this of all days, but worse, the precious moment she had deprived Abuela of through her obstinance. If not for Lina's insistence on dressing as she had, her grandmother might have come with her tonight. Might have been there to greet the spirits of her daughter—Lina's mother—and her grandson, whom neither of them had ever seen among the living; of course, if not for Papa's goggles, of which Abuela most definitely did *not* approve, perhaps neither of them would have been blessed with that sight.

Lina moved to where her grandmother stood before the oferenda. "Please, Abuela. Don't worry about that. We can take care of it tomorrow."

"Nonsense. It is shamefully in disarray."

Lina closed her mouth on her pointless argument, lips pressing in a thin line. She leaned her scythe against a nearby tree and bent to straighten up the altar as her grandmother wished before laying out their straw pallets for sleeping beside the grave, as the other families around them had already done. It would be an uncomfortable night, but it showed honor to the spirits of their loved ones to spend these precious hours in their presence before Death's shroud separated them once more, until the next year.

"The food…" Abuela called out, her voice rife with censure. "Why have you not placed the food on the oferenda? Ay, dios mios! Who will do this *properly* when I am gone?"

Frantic, Lina glanced around in the dark for her basket, dropped in the battle with the evil spirit that had stolen her father's form, whom she had vanquished with the help of Lady Death herself. Puzzled, Lina found the basket sitting nearby as if set down neatly and not dropped. As she knelt to pick it up, a gentle rustle reached her ears, along with a faint, familiar muttering she thought never to hear again.

Her breath trapped within her throat, she opened the basket and peered inside.

Satiny darkness and the faint gleam of a polished brass cowl stared back.

Gasping, Lina nearly tumbled back in shock.

Beltran. Her father's crow. His spirit's prison. Still wearing the cowl Papa had engineered to work with the goggles Lina wore, allowing the wearer to glimpse across the Veil to the spirit realm. Just hours before, Lina had cradled the crow as her scythe severed its life's bonds and set her father's soul free. And yet, that wicked beak now darted out and lightly pinched her finger as it had so often before. Lina laughed a startled laugh before raising her gaze to the heavens. She sent a prayer of thanks to Santa Muerte, for surely only she could have restored the crow. But why? For a moment, Lina would swear she saw a satisfied grin beneath a crown of roses among the branches overhead, followed by a shimmer of rich blue velvet fluttering out of sight.

"The food, niña, now!"

Flinching at the impatience in Abuela's tone, Lina ran a light finger over Beltran's crest, easing off the goggles and cowl, and then gently shooed him from the basket. He fluttered easily to a nearby tree branch so she could draw out the pan de muertos, roasted goat, and huevos con nopales she and Abuela had prepared earlier for the oferenda feast. Once she'd placed everything to her grandmother's satisfaction, Lina removed her mask and goggles—storing them in her now-empty basket—and she and Abuela lay their weary bones down to rest.

Lina woke surrounded by obsidian darkness. Though dew-sprinkled grass had cushioned her body what seemed like only moments before, now she stood. The rough stone beneath her feet seared her soles like bitter ice, and the breath of the surrounding hills bit with the chill of death. The path, however, glowed with golden light scattered before her, here thick, there faint, but always steady, always sure. Kneeling, she ran her hand over the ground, encountering the soft crinkle of marigold petals. As they continued to glow against the palm of her hand, she knew she traveled the Land of the Dead.

Sliding the petals into the pocket of her robe, she continued, keeping her feet to that path lest she be lost, her gaze searching the craggy distance ahead for the beacon that drew her. The flutter of wings swirled overhead, but she could not see feather or form to know the nature of the bird. Or what she *hoped* was a bird.

A burst of wind speared toward her through the angular hills, focusing her thoughts on her journey. It carried a raspy whisper, *"Come, mija, come to me. We must have words between us."*

Shivers rippled across Lina's skin beneath her worn cotton robe, but she followed the beckoning, somehow both climbing and descending at once along the golden path, her senses whirling but never losing the thread of that whisper leading her forward. Ahead, a cool white glow teased the horizon, picking out the hilly peaks looming sentinel over the path.

In the surrounding darkness, the air smelled and felt dry as dust while the clatter of bones danced in clicks and clacks, echoing off stony mounds. Sometimes close, sometimes fading off. And still, Lina continued on, a lifetime of wandering in a single instant. Instinct urged her forward though her gut rebelled. With each step, the icy chill climbed higher, caressing her toes, and then her ankles, and upward to her shins. Her heart quailed that it should be caught in that cold and final grip.

Yet, Lina continued.

The golden glow she followed paled, suddenly enveloped by a surge in the soft white light, like moonbeams on burnished bone. Lina's gaze relinquished the horizon to draw back, settling on the stately figure that appeared to stand before her, slender polished bone curving gracefully beneath a soft blue veil crowned by roses so deeply crimson they appeared black beneath the arch of the underworld, for surely that is where her path had taken her.

Lina's feet stopped without her feeling the cessation.

As she gazed in awe upon Santa Muerte, and not merely her reflection, Lina felt the flutter of wings beside her head buffeting her briefly as the wind of this place had not. She turned and locked gazes with Beltran. Lina gasped, her hand darting without thought to reach for the crow, gaining a peck for her ill manners. Was this a vision fed by this place, or was the sight for true? Lina could not say, but as she beheld the crow, she could not deny he — or the vision of him — watched her, his head cocking as corvids are wont to do, training one gleaming eye upon her, then the other, before giving a barking caw almost like a chuckle. The crow alit on her shoulder, ruffling his crest like the proud, cocky bird he was.

"Your eyes," she murmured in awe, her hand still raised, if respectfully distant from an actual touch. "She's restored your eyes..."

"Righting another wrong that should never have happened," the saintly figure murmured.

Lina turned away from the crow and settled her gaze on the death deity.

"Why are we here?"

"Because I wished it. And you answered."

Lina nodded, conceding the point, though Santa Muerte had not truly answered the question as intended. But having just been treated to a lesson in respect from Beltran, Lina merely waited in a semblance of patience for the creature of death and bone to speak her piece.

The glow from the goddess's ivory served well enough in the stead of muscle and flesh, a fair approximation of an amused grin gracing Santa Muerte's face at Lina's display of circumspection.

With a faint nod, the deity raised her hand, weaving her metacarpals through the darkness, the darting display of light and dark leaving impressions on Lina's mind like a shadow play depicting a battle.

"You have shown great courage, a strength of spirit worthy of any warrior of our people," Santa Muerte spoke into the silence. "As has your friend there. The two of you have done us a great service returning that demon to the underworld."

Lina shuddered at the mention of the creature.

"But more importantly, you freed a soul unjustly denied the afterlife."

Anger kindled in Lina's belly as Beltran's talons gripped her shoulder through her robe.

"Two died tonight, unjustly, *but you only brought one back.*" She set her stance and jutted her jaw, daring the deity to deny her claim, her father more important to her than her own self.

At Lina's challenge, embers flared bright in the pits of Santa Muerte's eye sockets as the luster of her brow dipped forward. "Make no mistake, niña, Vasco courted his death when he sought to breach a barrier he was not yet meant to cross. It was a kindness to free him to move on. More so than he deserved to reunite him with the love he sought so rashly. There are others even yet that do not enjoy that good fortune."

Lina frowned but grasped no point in arguing. It was, after all, that desire that had driven Papa like an obsession… guided his constant tinkering until he invented the spirit goggles in an effort to see into the spirit realm and reconnect with her mother.

Compassion softened Santa Muerte's expression.

"Do you have the courage to serve us, mija?"

The chill creeping up Lina's legs briefly surged through the rest of her.

Serve *Death*?

Her thoughts painted many pictures of what that might mean, projected in rapid-fire flashes across the landscape of her mind. Most of them made her heart quaver.

"Ahhh… *shshshshsh*…" Santa Muerte said, her fingers fluttering as if to shoo Lina's fears away. "Do not surrender your courage so swiftly. I do not look for a warrior to banish demons. I look for a guide both clever and compassionate, someone to usher the souls who have lost their way… or been blocked from it." She paused as if gauging Lina's understanding.

Lina drew a steadying breath and willed her eyes to relax from their widening.

"And so, I ask again," the goddess continued with a serene smile though she had no lips. "Have you the courage to serve us? Will you stand as Lady Death's angel?"

Icy fingers seemed to clutch Lina's heart. She would be a fool to think such service as Santa Muerte asked of her would always be so simple as just ushering souls. Could she commit her life to deal with the good and the bad of the spirit realm? There would be more moments like the night of Día de los Muertos and her confrontation with the damned soul who had stolen her father's body. But then she must also remember Papa as she had last seen him, the glimpse Santa Muerte had allowed her of his freed soul reflected in the mirror backing the oferenda, reunited at last with the spirits of her mother and her baby brother. To help such souls as these, how could Lina not serve? Abuela would never understand… but perhaps she need not know…

Beltran squawked and set his talons, fluttering his wings for balance as Lina abruptly straightened, then slowly nodded.

Santa Muerte reached out, and Angelina did likewise.

As their fingers intertwined, the glow surrounding them brightened, then flared, banishing the obsidian darkness.

Lina jerked upright out of slumber, her hands clutched in tight fists and her breath coming at a rapid pace. Abuela muttered and rolled away, surprisingly making no noise on her straw pallet. Closing her eyes, Lina lifted her face to the morning breeze as other families began to stir around them. After a moment, her breathing calmed, and her hands loosened.

From her fingers tumbled a slender bone, brilliant and white, with a subtle glow she only noticed in the corner of her eye. A finger bone. With trembling hands, she reached to pick it up again.

Not a dream, then, she thought. *Not a dream.*

The import struck her like a blow, leaving her again without breath. Gripping the finger bone tight, Lina rose quietly, her gaze searching the nearby trees for the crow. As if summoned by her thoughts alone — or possibly just her motion — he flew toward her, settling on a tall monument a few feet away.

"Beltran," she murmured, then shook her head. "No… no… a new life calls for a new name, don't you think? Something fitting to our calling…"

The crow cawed softly, bobbing in the jerky way crows did, then cocking his head to watch her from one newly restored eye.

Lina cocked her head back and stared at him a moment, then releasing a slow, even breath, she whispered, "Ujier… you are Ujier" — *Usher* — "and I am Angel, may we ever live up to those names."

With that, she slid the bone into the pocket of her robe, lest she lose it, drawing a sharp breath as her hand encountered flower petals. Shaking her head, she put the contents of her pocket from her thoughts and turned to the oferenda. Abuela still slept, and in the nearby woods lived those with no other home and little but what they could forage to eat. She took up her basket and placed the food inside, then wended her way beneath the trees until she encountered clear encampments to gift with her offerings. Above her head, Ujier winged through the branches, cawing in clear pleasure at his restored sight.

When she returned, Abuela had gone, leaving everything behind for Angel to manage.

Grumbling beneath her breath, she placed the now-cold candles from the altar in a line across each pallet and rolled them up, sliding them into her basket without filling it. Then she took the rest of the items from the altar and nestled them inside, glad to have already disposed of the food. The basket packed, she glanced around to ensure she had forgotten nothing. Content with how she had left the gravesite, she hefted the basket over her arm, took up her scythe, and whistled Papa's special whistle to summon Ujier. Or, at least, to let him know she made her way home. The crow would decide on his own whim if he joined her.

Wisps teased the corner of her vision as she traveled the path. Aether? Or spirits? Angel could not say, but given her father's goggles rested at the bottom of her basket, she found it disturbing to have seen either unaided. But then, it only made sense that Santa Muerte would equip her servant with the necessary tools to carry out her charge. Angel's thoughts went to the bone and flower petals in her pocket, and a shiver danced across her shoulders. What had she agreed to?

And how, precisely, was she to do as the goddess bid?

Angel still had no answer after the long walk home.

As she approached their hacienda, she frowned. She had expected to overtake Abuela on the road, but there had been no sight of her. Now that Angel was home, things felt too quiet, the air taut, as if waiting, the chickens still in their coop. She leaned the scythe next to the door and set her basket just inside.

"Abuela?" she called out. "*Abuela*, is all well?"

Silence rang as her answer.

With a huff, Angel searched from room to room, her nose twitching at a faint, sour smell she could not identify. The odor grew stronger as she neared her grandmother's closed door until Angel's stomach spasmed in protest. She swallowed hard and dropped her mouth open rather than breathe through her nose. "*Abuela*? Please answer me…"

Again, silence.

Angel raised her hand to knock but stilled, listening hard for any sound. At first, she barely noticed as soft tears trickled from her eyes. For a long moment, she looked down at the knob before reaching out to turn it. As soon as the door opened, little green flies filled the air.

"No! *Nonono!*" Angel cried as she rushed inside though she gagged and choked on the smell. She fell to her knees beside Abuela's bed, her hand reaching out to clutch her grandmother's dress. "No!" she sobbed, and then there were no words, only tears.

Angel woke to the sound of banging from the kitchen, echoed by banging in her head. She groaned and shifted, not knowing why she slept on the floor, or why her face ached, or why she could not breathe through her stuffed nose.

But only for as long as it took her to look up and see the lightly mottled hand hanging over the edge of the bed.

As the memories came crashing back to Angel, the banging continued.

Frowning, Angel scrambled to her feet and out of the room, her hands fisted and a snarl on her lips. With no care for silence, she burst into the kitchen, ready to battle with whoever intruded on her mourning.

She stopped stock still.

She swayed.

Abuela stood by the stove angrier than Angel had ever seen her before in life, and though she touched nothing, the pots hanging from their hooks swung wildly, banging against their neighbors as if some unseen hand tried to yank them down. As if her *grandmother* tried to yank them down.

"Abuela…" Angel whispered, her voice broken.

Slowly, the spirit turned, anger and fear and confusion darting violently in her gaze.

The pots banged louder.

Thickening tendrils of aether wreathed her grandmother's form.

Angel leaned her head against the doorjamb. "Oh, *Abuela*…"

The spirit remained silent, glowing shimmers trailing down her grandmother's cheeks like tears.

They stayed that way for a long time.

"Who will do this *properly* when I am gone?" Abuela's spirit wailed, the sound wispy and hollow in a way Angel hadn't noticed earlier at the gravesite, though clearly, Abuela's passing had taken place sometime just after Angel had left for the festivities nearly two days before.

Sighing, Angel rested her head against the door and tried to think. She had scarcely expected to begin her service to Santa Muerte so soon or in such a personal way. Where did she even begin?

With a firm grip on the doorjamb, she climbed to her feet, more conscious than ever of her rumpled cotton robe. As she tried to smooth it down, her hand brushed the pocket. She stilled. Held her breath. Reached into the pocket and pulled out the finger bone and a handful of marigold petals. Both glowed.

Could it be that simple?

Slowly, Angel approached her grandmother with her hand held out.

Abuela's spirit glanced down, clearly not comprehending.

The pots resumed their banging.

Angel groaned and thrust her hand forward before she could think about what she did.

Spirit and flesh intersected, and though the otherworldly items glowed even brighter, all else remained unchanged. Angel's flesh crackled with sudden, intense cold.

Giving her granddaughter a frigid look, Abuela retreated in a swirl of misty aether, not gone but no longer visible.

The barest of tears trickled down Angel's cheeks as she stared at the contents of her hand. A finger bone. Marigold petals. Both still shimmered with an otherworldly glow, though now muted. Somehow, they had to be the key to guiding Abuela's spirit to her rest. Angel slid the items back into her pocket before collecting the scythe and her basket from the entranceway and trudging into her father's workshop… *her* workshop, now.

She set her burdens to the side and firmly closed the door. Though none remained to care, she drew out her old tarp and tacked it over the doorframe as she used to do so Abuela would not know she worked late into the night, as her father had been inclined to do. The tarp helped deaden the smell, but not as much as Angel had hoped.

She moved to the workbench and lay the contents of her pocket across the well-used surface. Then she reached up and, one by one, drew her father's journals down from their shelf. In all of his studies of aether and the afterlife, there must be something he had learned that would help her.

A persistent caw from outside pulled Angel from her current journal. Her neck creaked as she turned to look, evidence she had immersed herself in her search longer than she'd expected.

Rising, Angel stretched the kinks from her back and shoulders, then moved across the room. With stiff fingers, she undid the latch on the window, then lifted the sash, pushing one shutter wide. Fresh air flowed over her, clearing her head—and the room—of the persistent stench she'd yet to address. As she stood there, breathing deep of the clean air, Ujier glided into the room. Showing off, he fluttered to his usual perch—as he had been unable to do just the day before—and began to preen.

"What do I do, pequeño?" *Little one.*

The crow made low, soothing sounds deep in his throat but merely continued to groom.

Angel huffed and returned to the journals, leaving the window open despite the growing chill as the sun set. Reaching over, she lit the oil lamp and continued to read until the oil was spent.

As the room fell dark and only moonlight lit her way, Angel settled on the cot her father kept in the corner and tried to sleep but found herself too weary to rest. Laying there in the overwhelming silence, Angel silently recited the rosary for her grandmother's soul.

Angel woke to bright light streaming through the window. And her grandmother.

Abuela stood over the cot where Angel lay, a scowl on her face and accusation in her gaze.

"I wasn't tinkering," Angel muttered sullenly as she sat up, hearing *'Aleta Angelina Fabricio!'* in her head, if not aloud. "I was trying to find a way to *help* you."

The ghost turned and disappeared through the still-shrouded door.

And the banging resumed.

Groaning, Angel flopped back down on the cot and squeezed her eyes shut as she wished she could close her ears. Silently, she cried out to Santa Muerte for help.

Perhaps she imagined it. Perhaps not. In either case, soft words drifted through her thoughts.

You have the key. Now you must find the door.

Angel's eyes snapped open, her thoughts focused. She scrambled from the cot and over to where the most recent journal still lay. All of Papa's research had been focused on peering across to the other side. Windows. Not doors. But windows — or some of them, anyway — could be opened. Under the right conditions, aether let one see through to the realm of the dead, as Papa's goggles had already proven, but looking through was quite different from passing through. It all began with aether, though, and thanks to the goddess, Angel could now see aether.

Everywhere.

It had taken her father so long to perfect his goggles because he could not see that essence, only understand it in theory. But somewhere in his books, she had read of the device he had used to harvest the aether that had proven the key to spirit sight. Fortunately, the journal had included sketches. Thumbing through until she found the entry she sought, Angel examined those sketches, then delved into the cabinets and shelves, looking for the infernal thing.

She would have immediately known where to look if she had been thinking clearly.

Under the circumstances, however, she felt she should be forgiven for her unclear thoughts.

She found the device on the shelf over the workbench, where two brass-studded leather cases that had housed the goggles resided. Climbing atop the workbench, she hauled the device down, taking particular care not to drop it, even as the ruckus from the kitchen unexpectedly grew louder. Carefully, she opened the case, removing a peculiar bellows-like object attached to copper condenser coils on one end and a small glass receptacle on the other.

"Oh… that will never do," she muttered, eying the chamber barely bigger than a thimble. While the size made complete sense given the purpose her father had intended for the aether, there was no way such a small amount would constitute a door.

Grabbing a graphite stick and a piece of scrap parchment, Angel began to sketch, visualizing an aether window and how such a mechanism would work. First, she needed two panes of glass between which she must trap the psychopompic essence. Second, a gasket to seal the panes, and third, a flexible tube to replace the thimble receptacle attached to the billows, which could then be fed into her glass-paned gas chamber.

It took several attempts once she gathered her materials from among her father's supplies. A gum-based seal proved insufficient on its own, but an outer barrier of melted wax held quite nicely, and likewise, a waxed leather tube appeared sound enough for her purposes.

In theory, anyway.

The structure held, and she'd engineered a simple wooden frame to hold it steady, but she had yet to engage the device. Humming in an attempt to drown out the banging, Angel engaged the psychopompic pump.

At first, nothing happened, but slowly an iridescent cloud formed between the precious sheets of glass. It swirled and pulsed and seemed inclined to take shapes, though Angel could not identify what those shapes were meant to be.

Finally, the chamber appeared full… almost opaque… with the volume of gas she'd captured. In theory, she had her door. Or a window, anyway, and were the two so drastically different in the end?

At her back, Ujier cawed.

She jumped as the crow soared to the top of the doorjamb and tugged the tarp free.

Angel gasped at the sudden influx of stench.

She really needed to deal with the body. But first, to save the soul!

On impulse, she began reciting the rosary once more as she carefully gathered up a fistful of marigold petals and laid a clear trail from her aether window to the door and then through it.

"Abuela," she called, but there was no answer, or any sight of her grandmother's spirit, though Angel could sense she hovered nearby. "*Abuela!*"

The house took on a sullen atmosphere.

"*Who will take care of you when I'm gone?*" Abuela whispered. Angel more felt the words than heard them as they wafted through the hacienda, filling every room with an expectant air.

"I will," Angel answered.

Her grandmother scoffed, and Angel felt it to her bones.

"I will," she repeated. "I *must*. You can't help me now."

Pressure built like a pending thunderstorm.

No grandmother would ever concede to not being needed, whether they could actually help or not. Angel's Abuela was no different. Thinking quickly, Angel raised the point guaranteed to soothe any grandmother's wounded pride. "You helped raise me well. Now… Mama is waiting. *Maximo* is waiting." She desperately hoped her words were not false.

The banging from the kitchen slowly faded to silence.

Abuela drifted closer, her form gaining definition as her "foot" connected with the marigold path. Scarcely daring to breathe, Angel closed her eyes and gripped the finger bone tightly, visualizing the window… *her* aether window sliding up.

Her eyes flew open as she heard Abuela gasp with joy.

There, framed by aether and glass, stood Maximo, his tiny spirit body bouncing with joy as he waited to meet his grandmother. Seeing Angel, he lifted his hand and waved.

More tears brimmed, though Angel could not believe she had any left. A smile tugged her lips wide as she waved back. Then she waited. For a long moment, no one moved, then Abuela slowly turned to glance over her shoulder, speaking the words Angel hadn't realized she desperately needed.

"I love you, mija. This isn't your fault."

Then Abuela stepped forward, and the aether flared, leaving Angel and Ujier to mourn in peace.

Ala al-Din and the Cave of Wonders

Based on Aladdin and the Lamp

Come, Best Beloved, and sit you by my feet. I shall tell you a tale such as sister Scheherazade could have scarce imagined… a tale oft told but little known. A tale of a foolish young man born seemingly of humble means but destined for glory and betrayal and, yes, Child of Adam, great love, though that is a tale for another day.

The night is for the telling of tales of which the morning may bear Truth. In the oldest of days and ages and times, there was, and there was not, a great evil that reached across the desert and beyond…

On this day, as with any other, Ala al-Din lounged against the low stone wall which edged Kashgar's famed bazaar, chin lifted and eyes half-closed, doing his best to appear to have no care in the world. In truth, he peered beneath his lids at a group of foreigners from the west gathered at the gate, bustling like industrious seed beetles as they set up intriguing paraphernalia to take photographs of the famed market, or so he had been told. Deep inside, a part of him yearned to move closer even as it ached that such things were lost to him. Worth it, to return home and tell his mother all he had seen, only these were British soldiers, part of an expedition led by a man called Sir Douglas Forsyth. Such important men as that would not welcome his presence.

Frowning, he scratched gently at a bit of dry skin on the stump of his right wrist and adjusted his skull cap, turning his gaze away from temptation, as he should have done at age eleven when he'd tried unsuccessfully to steal extra food so his mother would eat.

Ala al-Din resettled himself against the wall, angling his head away as he basked in the warm sun and the cool breeze, glad he had chosen a place upwind from those selling livestock. If only he could so easily avoid the chatter of the young boys around him. Most waited eager and hopeful to earn some coin for delivering messages or purchased goods for those desiring to shop unburdened. Ala al-Din wished only to be left in peace, or so he told himself. Let them run from one end of the oasis town to the other and back again all the hours of the day.

Not he. Why, when no one would trust either messages or goods to his care?

Of course, this is not to say he didn't come to his feet with all the others when opportunity neared. It would not do to be seen as idle, even if he held little hope for his effort. He straightened as purposeful footsteps approached, but did not push forward, as the others did, yammering and bouncing as if to display the wealth of energy they possessed, surely making them best suited for the task on offer.

Ala al-Din tensed, slouching to seem smaller and younger, just in case, as a tall man with skin like dark sandstone strode toward them. A finely knit white kufi covered his head, and a rich blue djellaba flowed around his body. If Ala al-Din had to guess, he would say this man hailed from Africa… likely Maghreb, given his manner of dress. Such foreigners were no odd sight along the Silk Road, any more than the British were. Kashgar was a hub of trade, and merchants the world over journeyed there, traveling by caravan or airship, and once, a most magnificent contrivance he'd learned was a Selden auto-mobile prototype. And Ala al-Din had little to do but watch them.

His attention must have lingered too intently. The westerner locked eyes with him, or so it seemed. Ala al-Din shrank back even further, disturbed by the stranger's intent gaze. Let one of the others collect the coin they were so eager for. Ala al-Din would wait and comb the ground on his way home for any cash dropped in the day's commerce, as was his practice so that his mother would not question how he filled his hours. He could hardly confess to her that no one would entrust him with their goods, once they had seen his stump, assuming — not incorrectly — that he had been punished for thievery. Why would that day be any different?

Except the westerner pushed past all the others, coming to stand firmly and with determination before Ala al-Din.

"You, boy. What is your name?"

Warily, Ala al-Din tucked his arms behind him, hiding the fact that one sleeve of his coarse cotton khalat had been pinned over an empty wrist. He looked up into those powerful eyes and found himself locked in the man's gaze as if compelled.

"Your name…"

"Ala," he muttered. "Ala al-Din."

"And your father?"

A scowl twisted Ala al-Din's expression as he fought the impulse to answer and lost. "Mustafa, the artificer."

Satisfaction flared in the stranger's gaze. "Allah be praised!"

Ala al-Din flinched as the man threw his arms around him, lifting him up as the other runners scattered like startled swan geese, some sulking, others already looking for the next to offer coin.

The stranger set Ala al-Din down but kept a grip on his shoulders.

"My boy! I am Kaddour, your uncle."

"Your…" Ala al-Din's words stumbled as his thoughts swirled in confusion. His mother had told him his father had had a brother, but that he had died. "He's dead. My father."

Kaddour frowned and peered intently into Ala al-Din's eye before nodding with a semblance of sorrow. "As he believed I was, but as you see, I am not. Let us go to your mother and share with her these good tidings."

Ala al-Din shrugged just enough that Kaddour's hands fell away, then he nodded, though unease threaded his belly. Together they left the bazaar, and Ala al-Din led the way to the street nearby where craftsmen set up their workshops, his steps growing more reluctant the closer they drew. At one time, his father had a shop right on the street, with a proud metalwork sign proclaiming 'Mustafa the Artificer' hung above the door. Now… Well, now, his mother's finances allowed her a tiny room on an alley off the street, and a cloth banner embroidered with 'Tahmina the Tinker' tacked beside the door. Ala al-Din and his mother slept in a tiny alcove at the back, able to afford nothing more.

When Kaddour saw the banner bearing not Al al-Din's name, but his mother's, and the threadbare tapestry draping the entrance, his brow furrowed, and his head cocked ever so slightly to the side. "Surely my brother provided better for his family. Did he not at least pass on his craft?" While the words were solicitous, Ala al-Din would swear that the tone held barely veiled pity.

He frowned and tugged at his handless arm.

Before he could comment, the curtain rings jingled as Kaddour swept the cloth aside.

"Welcome…" his mother called out, only to trail off at the sight of him and the stranger with him. "Can… can I help you?"

The man looked around as if tallying the value of all he saw, and finding it wanting, his nose wrinkling at the faint scent of dust and dank that permeated the space, no matter how they aired it. Ala al-Din's muscles tensed, and a phantom tingle danced about the end of his stump as if his missing hand fisted. Supposed family, or not, Kaddour had no call to cast even silent aspersions on his mother's efforts. She kept a neat shop, with well-crafted offerings, within the best of her meager means. At that thought, Ala al-Din's belly soured with guilt. Had he not been a foolish and lazy boy, he might be hale and whole this day, and he and his mother would not be reduced to sorting trash piles in the alleys of Kashgar for usable parts when their coffers ran dry.

"Apa…" — mother — Ala al-Din began only to have his words trampled.

"Allah willing, I can help you, my sister," Kaddour answered with a brief bow, stepping into the shop and leaving Ala al-Din to follow behind.

His mother's confusion deepened into a frown, and she turned her gaze on Ala al-Din.

"Kaddour-aka came upon me in the market, he says he is my father's brother."

Her eyes widened briefly before narrowing. "And how would he know this?"

The man stepped forward, his arm gesturing as if to draw her eye, rather than direct it.

"Please, Tahmina, does your son not look the image of my brother, Mustafa, in his younger days?" Kaddour pointed toward two pictures above Tahmina's workbench — a photograph of Ala al-Din's parents on their wedding day, next to a daguerreotype of his grandparents on theirs. "Even as I am a reflection of what my brother would have been had he grown older?" The westerner held no tension in his body as if his words were given and irrefutable. And perhaps they were as Ala al-Din watched a shadow of doubt waft across his mother's gaze. Her eye narrowed and she worried the barest edge of her lip as if torn between belief and disbelief.

"Mustafa did travel from afar before settling in this place. And you do bear some passing resemblance," she murmured, her tone conflicted, as caution and hope fought for control. "What is it that you wish?"

"Merely to assist my brother's family in their time of need, now that I have found them. To restore them to the honorable station they would have held had he not been taken from us too soon."

While Ala al-Din could take no exception at the man's specific words, faint warnings echoed in his thoughts at the skillful manner in which his supposed uncle emphasized them with subtle precision, fanning the flame of his mother's hope until it flared with more strength than her caution. Of course, she toiled all day in this alleyway hovel, while Ala al-Din spent his days observing all manner of speech and careful maneuvering among those frequenting the market. He exercised his suspicion more often than she, while his hope had been trampled and smothered until a mere shadow of her own.

And still. He wanted to believe, and so he remained silent as his mother smiled and offered to fetch tea from their precious and limited store.

And thus, in a mere matter of days, Kaddour—with his own hands—helped them sort through their meager belongings. Ala al-Din and his mother were swept from their alley and into a storefront on the very street where the famed Mustafa had once plied his trade, with proper household quarters above the shop. By what means it had been procured Ala al-Din could not say and did not want to know. He was hesitant to question their good fortune, for his mother's sake.

He smiled and watched on as his mother fluttered through the shop like a jeweled songbird in her new khalat and richly colored rumol. She darted from the workbench where Mustafa's journal sat in place of honor—filled with designs he'd made and those he'd only imagined—to the various shelves, laughing as she ran her fingers through baskets of gears and over spanners and calipers and all manner of delicate tools and materials meant for fine workings of the sort that would see them well-appointed for years to come. They suddenly had the materials for nearly any job, be it clockworks or automata or similar intricate-but-frivolous contraptions the wealthy commissioned to lord them over others, rather than the work-a-day pumps and locks and cruder workings that had been all they could manage with scavenged parts.

Ala al-Din tugged at the sleeve of *his* new khalat, made of colorfully patterned cashmere, with embroidery at the cuffs, and reached up to brush his fine, white skull cap. Though of higher quality, he could not call the new clothing more comfortable than the old, as self-conscious as it made him feel, as if he pretended to higher than his station, though his uncle scoffed at such concerns when Ala al-Din voiced them.

"What use can you be to me if you wander Kashgar looking like a beggar?"

If not for the joyful and carefree way Tahmina explored the shop, every so often exclaiming with glee, Ala al-Din would have walked away from Kaddour without hesitation. To see her so happy, with the weight of worry lifted from her brow… There was much a son would bear to preserve a mother's well-being, no matter the doubts that might niggle his mind.

"Come, come, Ala," his uncle said, tugging him from the shop before Ala al-Din could protest. "Let us visit the neighboring shops and introduce you around."

Ala al-Din frowned. Not only were these the people who had known him all his life… or at least for the beginning of it… but why should *he* matter? Any hope of his building delicate machinery had died six years ago when his hand had been taken, and the memories of what his father had taught him had faded to near uselessness. He hung back until his half-empty sleeve stretched between them, and Kaddour finally realized he no longer followed like an obedient child. Once the man stopped and turned, Ala al-Din pulled his arm from Kaddour's grip.

With a nod, he said, "I bid you a good day, but I am needed here." He then pivoted around to return to the shop and help his mother. As soon as he turned, the newly hung sign above the door caught his eye, proclaiming to all Kashgar that this was the establishment of Ala al-Din the Artificer.

"What? What is this? That cannot be. It is not true."

"What do you know, boy?"

"I have not been a boy for a very long time," Ala al-Din muttered, glaring over his shoulder at Kaddour, his brow furrowed.

"What would happen, do you imagine," the westerner growled, leaning in close to Ala al-Din's face, "were we to advertise Tahmina the Tinker above that shop?"

Mulishly, Ala al-Din set his heels and his jaw likewise, not backing away.

"Answer me!"

"My mother would get the recognition she deserves for her work."

"Wrong! She would be treated as if she still did business in that hovel in the alley. Her wares would be overlooked because the custom would have already made up their minds."

Ala al-Din wanted to argue, but unfair is not untrue.

"And why my name and not your own?"

Something flared in Kaddour's gaze, heat and smoke and smoldering embers. His tone, however, remained calm, almost dismissive. "My talents lay elsewhere than the mechanical, boy, and none know me here. Better to build on their familiarity with your family."

Rather than fan the flame, Ala al-Din remained silent, nodding in acknowledgment and nothing more. His recalcitrance was not lost on Kaddour.

"I will do my best for you and your mother, Ala, but you must trust me."

Every instinct screamed at him not to do so, but at his back, Ala al-Din could still hear his mother's hums as she reordered the shop to her liking, every so often punctuated by a delighted giggle. How could he take that from her? And for what cause? Other than the deceit of the sign, Kaddour had done nothing out of order. And still, Ala al-Din held misgivings.

"Who will believe I can craft with one hand?"

Kaddour frowned briefly, before giving a slow nod and reaching out to guide Ala al-Din back toward the shop. "There is truth in this. We shall deal with that first."

Overly conscious of the mechanical hand strapped to his stump — a simple hand-shaped clamp crafted by his mother, from designs found in his father's journal — Ala al-Din followed his uncle through the city streets and into the market. They strolled seemingly without purpose, Kaddour stopping to examine copper fittings at one stall, and *tsk*ing over ill-cut gears at another, but always taking a moment to introduce Ala al-Din to the merchants and ask about their wares, while throwing in a random question or two about the countryside, or the Silk Road, or the bands of nomads traveling the sands. At first, Ala al-Din dismissed it as idle chatter, until he noticed a pattern in the questions, slight variations, but always fundamentally the same, as if Kaddour sought something but didn't quite know where. Ala al-Din's mind puzzled over it until he could remain silent no longer.

"What is it you search for?" he asked, as Kaddour sorted through a bin of spare cogs and gears and twisted coils of copper wire as if treasure might lay beneath, but all the while asking his peculiar questions.

If Ala al-Din were not so close, he would have missed the hiss his uncle swallowed as he snapped his head around to fix Ala al-Din with a hard stare. "Nothing, boy, I merely seek to familiarize myself with the region where I will be making my home."

Straightening, Kaddour turned away from the merchant's wares as if they hadn't moments before held him seemingly riveted. Without another word, he strode off with purpose, leaving Ala al-Din to hurry after.

He would have scarce caught up if his uncle hadn't stopped abruptly. Ala al-Din stopped a short distance away to observe as Kaddour settled on a short stone wall near one of the storytellers that regaled the crowd for whatever coin they would toss her. Though he pretended to adjust his sandal, Ala al-Din noticed the cant to his uncle's head, the ear angled to hear the tale being told, and the way his hands stilled in the middle of their task, as if to ensure it was not too quickly done. It had been some time since Ala al-Din had paid any attention to the tales told in the market, so he could not say what story the woman told, but as he moved closer, her words wove a picture of a hidden cavern far beneath the desert where trees bore jewels in lieu of fruit and a Shah's treasure waited to be returned to his rightful heirs. She described great metal beasts and dangers untold, the sulfurous stench of demons, and an ageless beauty bound by invisible chains, guardian of the ages. *"Are you Ins or are you Djinn?"* he heard her murmur in the telling of her tale, her voice exotic, though her features were no different from those born to call this place home. Whether by nature or artifice, she held her audience enthralled.

Ala al-Din wanted to laugh at such fanciful descriptions, only Kaddour had given up all pretense and hung on the woman's words.

With an uneasy feeling, Ala al-Din slowly withdrew, making his way back to the shop that bore his name, but not to his credit.

In the dark hours before dawn, Ala al-Din woke to a violent shaking of his shoulder. He reared up and drew away, a cry on his lips and his empty sleeve flinging out as if it still bore a fist, only to have his shout muffled by a rough hand and his blow batted away.

"Stop it," Kaddour hissed. "Get up and come with me."

When Ala al-Din tried to speak, the westerner pressed his hand firmer. "Do you wish to wake your mother? To give her more worry than you already have in life?"

With a glower, Ala al-Din slowly shook his head.

"If you come with me, it will ensure her continued good fortune." Though his tone bore no threat, the implication hung heavy in the air.

Ala al-Din rose from his pallet and dressed in silence. Though he could not say why, he strapped on his likeness of a hand before following his uncle downstairs and through the silent city streets. They left with few to note their passing, venturing out beyond the oasis and into the desert proper.

As they traveled the sands, he had call to be grateful for the brand-new khalat holding the warmth to his body. This close to the cold season, the night had grown chilled with the setting of the sun.

"Uncle," Ala al-Din called out, "where do we go?"

"Shh!"

"It is cold, and I am tired, if there is no purpose to this journey I would as soon return to my slumber."

Kaddour turned and stalked back to where Ala al-Din had stopped, his expression the epitome of solicitous.

"I need your help retrieving something I have lost. Something taken from me. Once I have it, none of us need work again unless we chose to do so. Can you not imagine how that would be? No more loitering in the market to be shunned by those seeking runners, no more make-work for Tahmina, who may choose what to build at her pleasure. Would not your father, Mustafa, desire this?"

"What is this thing we seek?"

"An intricate beast of the air, a mechanical falcon crafted in the finest of handwork, with delicately formed gears the size of a pea and thin plates sheathing its clockworks in the seeming of banded feathers. And for the eyes, two rare black diamonds swirling with the steam inside."

Ala al-Din considered Kaddour's words. While the working sounded exquisite, he could not fathom how such a thing would accomplish all that his uncle promised. "The market is full of such machinations. What makes this one of such note?"

In the dark, it was difficult to see the truth of Kaddour's expression. Did his features shift and harden, or was it an illusion of moonlight and shadow? He remained silent overlong, but finally… "To me, its value is beyond measure. Made long ago by your own father's hand, a present for me, snatched away before it could be given."

Ala al-Din frowned. His father had been gifted, and his talent had done well for them, but never could he remember such workings as Kaddour claimed. Not even written down in his father's journal, where he had tracked all his designs to aid with future innovations. But then, who was he to dispute Kaddour's claims? By the time Ala al-Din was born, his father's workings had turned toward practical designs.

"How will this thing accomplish what you claim?"

"Why, my boy…" The pause was not long, but Ala al-Din noted it… as if Kaddour searched the recesses of his mind for an answer without question. "Can you not imagine the acclaim the shop will garner with a machination of this magnificence on display? The custom would come in droves such that you… your mother could choose among them to her heart's desire and be paid so handsomely that it would matter not who was turned away."

Oh, to have such coin. Ala al-Din thought longingly of the photography equipment used by the British expedition. With their finances restored, he might secure the like for himself. From what he had seen, photography was a skill he could learn with but one hand, particularly with his new prosthetic. And with Kaddour here to look after mother, perhaps Ala al-Din might venture out into the world — where his one well-meant indiscretion would no longer plague him — and capture its wonders on film.

"Come!" Kaddour barked. "We haven't much time."

They wandered a while longer, their path seemingly guided by the details garnered in the market, though mostly by the storyteller's tale. Finally, Kaddour stopped when the promise of the sun barely kissed the sky and made it blush. Before them lay a crumbled column, ancient stones weathered and worn smooth, once balanced high as if an archway to the desert, positioned on the edge of an oasis much smaller than the one Kashgar had grown around. Ala al-Din just stood there, awkward and uncomfortable, as his uncle searched the ground, for what only he knew. Finally, Kaddour straightened with a triumphant cry. Spinning back around, the westerner came close, fervor burning in his gaze as he gripped Ala al-Din by the shoulders in an echo of their first meeting.

"Listen, boy. Listen close. I am about to open the way we seek. You must remain silent and move swiftly, for only you can venture forth to find the treasure we are after."

Ala al-Din shook his head. "I do not understand. Why me?"

"Why, you are slighter than I and thus will fit through the passage."

Against such blatant fact, Ala al-Din could not argue. He nodded, and Kaddour turned back, arms raised until the drape of his robe obscured any view Ala al-Din may have had. The man muttered and shook and stamped on the ground… and nothing happened. Kaddour tried again, his voice louder, his tone more commanding. Still nothing.

Ala al-Din was puzzled at his behavior, and softly repeated the syllables he'd heard quite clearly the second time, rolling them around in his mouth before they whispered past his lips.

Suddenly, the earth rumbled and jumped beneath their feet.

"Ay!" Kaddour called out, stumbling back against the toppled stones and falling on his rear as the sand slid away to reveal a maul in the earth, rimmed with blunt stone, like teeth. "Go! Go, boy. Touch nothing but the falcon, or surely you will never return if you do. The guardian of the cavern is quite fierce."

With a nod, Ala al-Din stepped forward to the edge of the maul, staring down into the darkness. Before he could turn to ask how he should descend, a hard shove met with his back, and he tumbled down the hole.

When consciousness — if not sense — returned Ala al-Din rolled his aching body over to stare up at the circle of sky above him. Wheezing out a breath, he scrambled to his feet, the opening taunting him, just barely three feet out of reach. If his limbs were all sound, he might have jumped up to catch the rim and pull himself free. Not today. A single beam of light sliced through the darkness. Where the light hit, it revealed Ala al-Din looking rumpled and dusty but, for the most part, unharmed, and beneath his feet, a floor mosaic of precious gems. He was about to call out to his… uncle when a frantic thought pierced the fog shrouding his mind.

You must remain silent…

As he moved off down the passage, the darkness receded. Not completely, but enough that, with squinting, Ala al-Din could just make out his way. He took care not to shuffle or scuff, taking only slow, sure steps lest he wake whatever guardian lurked. The barest scratch of dirt on tile taunted his ear, and unseen motes of dust tickled his nose, but Ala al-Din made no sound as he moved forward with deliberation, straining to hear any noise to betray another's presence.

He heard nothing but his own strained breath.

The further he traveled down the passage the more the darkness receded, giving way to the promise of twilight as a faint but increasing splatter of glow adorned the walls. Ala al-Din reached out and delicately brushed the points of light, encountering a layer of soft tufts that darkened where he touched. He pulled his hand away, rubbing his fingertips together, marveling at the faint shimmer left behind with the barest hint of moisture. Lichen. He had heard tales, though he could not say if they were true, of long-ago miners chipping the surface layer of lichen-covered rocks to make crude lanterns where they dare not carry flame.

The deeper he traveled into the cavern the brighter the passage seemed until he could make out the arch of an opening expanding into a larger space that seemed to glow even brighter yet, with a subtle lavender hue. With caution, he crept forward, staying close to the stone wall, peering past the opening to a sight of true wonder.

A soft gasp escaped his lips.

The light flared brighter, and of a sudden, Ala al-Din felt pinned beneath the weight of a thousand stares. He dare not move, but his gaze darted about the chamber taking in the massive dome of the chamber braced by a latticework of brass-fitted glass tubes from which the light emanated. Beneath that stunning dome lay a treasure beyond Ala al-Din's imagine. Beyond his comprehension. Beyond his very dreams. Casks of gold and jewels and vessels with wax stoppers that might hold anything from rare spices to exotic scents. At the center of the trove stood a bejeweled throne — a broad platform beneath a canopy ornamented with two peacocks that bespoke a Persian influence. And surprisingly, along the edge of the trove, piled haphazardly, without regard, lay common goods as one would find in any market. He saw no sign of a falcon, clockwork or otherwise, though along the curved wall he could make out a string of what appeared to be mechanical camelids.

Scarcely the same thing.

On the far side of the chamber, however, past the treasure, Ala al-Din spied something most perplexing.

A workshop. As alike his father's as to be unmistakable.

Ala al-Din stepped forward into the light.

A sound began to build, like the hissing of the desert's fury as the sands themselves rose up to express their displeasure. From nowhere, a gust of hot air — the breath of a demon? — brushed wherever his skin lay bare, tugging his khalat and snatching away his skull cap. Swallowing his cry, he hurried to grab the covering back, stumbling among the treasure in his haste, disturbing it.

"Thief!" a voice called out, both harsh and melodious at once. It reverberated through the chamber, pinging off the glass and jangling the fine metalwork among the trove.

Memories of that long-ago day… the fear… the thrill… the panic as the guards seized him… worse, as the blade bit his flesh, then bone, despite his pleas and cries...

He reared away, fighting a grip that was not there. Something sharp caught his wrist, tugging, slicing. All flooded back, tearing a scream from the depths of Ala al-Din's heart.

A biting, metallic scent like rusted iron fanned his terror until then and now melded into one desperate nightmare as a hot trickle of blood dripped off his fingers.

A gasp sounded throughout the chamber, as soft and gentle as the first cry had been harsh. It held notes of wonder and not quite disbelief, but most of all, it held hope.

"Son of Persia… Blood of the Nadar Shah… Be still. Be welcome. Be at peace. Be healed."

A warmth suffused the cut on Ala al-Din's wrist as the lavender glow dimmed and swirled in soothing patterns, and a plume of violet vapor drifted in the glass cylinder above his head. Eyes formed as the plume took the shape of a beautiful woman made of smoke.

Ala al-Din's frantic breath slowed, then stilled, and his eyes widened. "Are you Ins or are you Djinn?" he murmured without thinking, though the answer was clear.

The vapor woman danced and laughed as if he'd been clever, her color brightening with her delight.

"We have waited long for the rightful heir."

Ala al-Din's eyes went wider still until pupil and iris were but concentric dots in a pool of white. His breath panted from his chest as he took in her words and made a frightening sense of them. Carefully, he climbed to his feet and stood clear of the legendary mounds. He may no longer listen to the tales in the market, but that did not mean he had not heard them. Who *hadn't* heard of the famed lost treasure of Nadar Shah, and his equally lost bloodline? Even as far east as Kashgar.

By sheer force of will, he stilled his heartbeat and slowed his breathing.

"No," he stated, not with force or fervor, but with solid, unwavering conviction. Such wealth, such obligation, such *risk* a treasure of that magnitude represented would build chains to shackle his dreams and desires. He had already lost one life and would not sacrifice another. "No," he repeated.

"I do not understand…"

"Such, I do not wish for myself. It is not a life, it is a procession, where the needs of all others dictate your steps"—here he held up his right arm—"I have not done so well with such choices."

"But…"

"I am certain I am not the only one, the shahs were said to sow nearly as much seed as farmers. Your kind is ageless, another will come along."

Ala al-Din turned and walked back down the passage, not stopping until he stood beneath the maul, squinting up at the bright blue sky.

Kaddour's head moved into view, occluding the light, his gaze maniacally eager. Unease gathered in Ala al-Din's belly. His own arguments echoed in his thoughts as he stared up at the embodiment of his fears.

"Where is it, boy? Hand me the Djinn!"

Ah, so that was what drove his uncle, dreams of limitless power enslaved to his every desire.

Ala al-Din squared his shoulders and held his head high.

"There is no mechanical falcon."

"Liar!" Kaddour growled, all semblance of benevolence leached from his expression.

"Come see for yourself, *uncle*."

"Stay there until you find it, *boy*," he hissed back before uttering a guttural string of words wholly unfamiliar to Ala al-Din, despite a lifetime living in a hub of global commerce.

"No! No!" he yelled over the strange syllables, leaping, his hands reached out to grab the lip of the maul, but unable to grip. "Damn you, Kaddour! May the fires of Jahannam burn you black for all eternity!"

His words had no effect save to punctuate his helplessness. As the final syllable fell from Kaddour's lips, a whirlwind swept in, burying the maul—and Ala al-Din—beneath the sands.

Ala al-Din seethed in the darkness for a very long time. Long enough his belly grumbled, long enough his bladder complained. Long enough, he began to notice the faintest of lavender glow.

"Djinni," he murmured. "Is it you he sought?"

"I do not know," she murmured back, strengthening her glow until Ala al-Din saw the single glass pipe leading back toward the cavern. "Perhaps."

"But no. He sent me to retrieve a clockwork falcon."

The glow flared until the antechamber lit up like a fever dream. "*What?*"

"A falcon. I was to take the falcon and nothing else."

"Shahin," the djinn uttered with a breath. "My brother, of sorts. He is no longer here. Please… you must warn him."

Ala al-Din narrowed his gaze, his suspicion newly rekindled. "I told you…"

"No! I do not seek to sway you… trap you. I cannot leave this place of my own accord, and if this sorcerer knows to target the falcon, he knows Shahin is bound to it. Please… it is a terrible thing for the djinn to be coerced."

He knew the feeling. And in that moment, Ala al-Din filled with an overwhelming sense of dread akin to the djinni's. How could he have forgotten? His mother. Alone and at Kaddour's mercy.

"I cannot," he said softly, true regret giving weight to his words. "I cannot leave my mother unprotected from my uncle…"

The lavender glow deepened to the purple of a bruise, cutting him off. "That one is no kin to you! He is a sorcerer from a far-off land, only eager to add to his power that of a djinn."

Ala al-Din frowned, torn as to what to do.

"I cannot be as you wish."

"My only wish now is that you warn my brother. Anything else is a concern for another day."

"But my mother…"

"And can you help her from here?"

A snarl twisted Ala al-Din's lips. At every turn, his hand forced… and he with but one of them.

"Can you free me?"

"Yes."

"Can you restore this?" He held up his handless arm.

A sense of unease filled the chamber as if a creature made of light and smoke could squirm.

"Can you?"

A soft huff faded into the stone walls.

"After a sort."

"Explain."

"I am a djinn, not a god. I cannot create flesh. I can take what has been crafted and refine it, give it grace and function and form, but not flesh and blood."

Ala al-Din latched on to the only word that mattered. "Function."

"After a sort," she repeated, reluctance drawing out her words. Her response stirred remembrance. Echoes of past dealings observed in the marketplace. Classic avoidance masked as cooperation. Canting his head slightly, he watched her as he asked his next question.

"Will you fix this?"

"I may or I may not."

Straightening, Ala al-Din stared direct at the djinn and uttered two words: "Fix it."

A moment of silence before she answered, "As you wish."

Light, a pale lilac, nearly white, descended in tendrils that wove around his prosthetic, caressing it, tracing the lines and joins, feeding through the gaps to illuminate the inside, light pushing out again through the seams until Ala al-Din fairly felt it pulse. Gradually, the glow faded. "Is it done?" he asked, his words taut with anticipation.

"See for yourself," she murmured, her glow dimmed, though he could not say from overuse or displeasure.

Nigh on holding his breath, Ala al-Din bent his will to flex the fingers, to flare them out flat as the clamp configuration would never allow. And as he wished it, so it was.

"Thank you," he breathed, his fingers still dancing before him as he studied them with awe.

Looking up to where she floated in the pipe—a mere spark of her former glory—he vowed, "I shall warn Shahin."

A faint pulse, and no more.

Worn, then, he answered for himself. And he settled down to nap until she was restored.

Ala al-Din woke next to a wooden bowl filled with gemstones nearly indistinguishable from plucked fruit: amber apricots and amethyst grapes, sapphires like perfect round blueberries plump with juice. He took up a ruby like a bright red cherry and marveled at the lapidary skill it would take to craft such a thing. Looking up to where the djinni had perched last night — day? he had lost track — he met her gaze, itself like onyx or black diamond.

"Thank you, but neither my teeth nor my belly is up to such fruit."

She nodded her concession. "These are to sustain you and your household by other means, now that your... *patron*... is disenfranchised."

"I was told to take nothing."

"Such warning does not apply to those of the blood, whether or not they seek to claim it. These are but a small portion of what is rightfully yours."

Rather than consider that temptation too closely, he offered her his own nod, then, remembering his promise, he asked, "My thanks. Have I leave to deliver these to my mother before I set out?"

The djinni frowned faintly upon him. "No need. Shahin will find you soon enough. Once sensed, your blood is like a beacon to those charged to serve... to *protect* the Afsharid dynasty."

A shiver coursed down his limbs as he wondered who else might take interest in his blood.

"Djinni, I wish to go home now."

If not for their new shop and restored good fortunes, Ala al-Din would have thought his encounter in the Cave of Wonders, and all that led to it, a fever dream. He had awoken in his bed with seemingly nothing out of order. The sound of his mother's singing drifted up from the workshop below, and his clothing lay waiting to be donned, but as Ala al-Din rose and began to put them on, each layer he lifted revealed the marvel of the magicked hand beneath. In fact, though the prosthetic had not yet been strapped on, the fingers clenched as if gripping his pants to pull them up. The garment in question fell from his left hand to puddle on the floor.

Ala al-Din reached for the prosthetic and affixed it to his stump with no measure of discomfort, other than a bit of leeriness. It sat comfortably with nary even an itch to annoy him as he went about his day.

"Allah, be praised," he murmured as he finished dressing and went downstairs to help his mother.

And thus, their days went on for several fortnights, with no mention between them of the transformed hand or the bowl of jewels hidden beneath the hearthstone against future need. The custom came, out of curiosity, if nothing else. Kaddour did not, more curious still. Ala al-Din held himself ready for the day the sorcerer surfaced, under no illusion he would just walk away. In the meantime, he applied himself to the study of Mustafa's journal, desiring to aid his mother as he had failed to do in the past. He had not her passion but did possess a measure of skill. They worked contently side by side. It felt good to have an honest claim to the sign above their shop, though still, he would have preferred his mother receive the recognition due her.

As memory faded into the background and routine relaxed his guard, there came a night when Ala al-Din ventured out after dark to deliver a newly completed commission bespoke by Yaqub Beg himself, Emir of Kashgaria, and for which, surely, they would receive no pay. He consoled himself with the knowledge that others would covet the prestige of possessing clockworks crafted by the Artificer to the Emir. And if not, they needed not the coin, having no desire for great wealth, beyond their needs.

Lost in his musings, Ala al-Din barely noticed the sound of shuffling in the street ahead of him as he wheeled his handcart toward the Emir's compound. When four figures emerged from the shadows to block his path, he stumbled to a halt, the cart clattering behind him as he dropped the handles to the ground.

Before he could react, or even speak, two others seized him from behind.

Within moments they dragged him away down an alley, leaving the cart abandoned in the street.

"What do you want of me?" he asked, not for the first time, though the thugs repeatedly ignored him, binding his hands behind him and pushing him to his knees. Ala al-Din did not resist. Even unbound, he could not have stood against five assailants, and escape was unlikely with so many to block his way.

"Time to make good on our agreement, boy."

Ala al-Din tensed at the familiar voice, cursing himself for letting down his guard. He remained silent as Kaddour emerged from the shadows to stand before him.

"And where is my falcon?" he asked.

Looking up to meet the westerner's eye, Ala al-Din did not bother to shield his hatred.

"There was no falcon," he answered, relieved his "uncle" had not asked about djinn, only the vessel, and so he could answer honestly.

"How did you escape?"

"I did not." And such was true. Escape implied action on his part.

Snarling, Kaddour chanted too low for the words to reach Ala al-Din's ears. As he did so, he raised his hand, his fingers curled. Ala al-Din gasped as that grip wrapped like a steel band around his throat. The sorcerer lifted him from the ground high enough that his legs dangled, without once touching him. He hung there and did not fight it.

"How did you escape!"

"I did not." Ala al-Din answered, his words strained. "I woke in my own bed."

The grip on his throat tightened, and still, he did not fight, merely holding Kaddour's gaze in defiance. To struggle would be to give the sorcerer satisfaction, and any futile efforts would only weaken Ala al-Din. Instead, he contorted his arms behind his back, his flesh hand twisting to unseat his prosthetic.

As they glared one another down, a strident cry sounded above. The scream of a bird of prey, unnatural in the night. For an instant, Kaddour's focus broke, his startled gaze snapped upward. Ala al-Din's feet hit the ground, as did his mechanical hand, and he pictured it scrabbling across the distance to seize the sorcerer by the throat. Swift and sure, it scurried. Before the man could react, it locked down tight in a crushing hold, cutting off the sorcerer's breath as he tried to resume his chanting. Ala al-Din shook off his now-loose bonds and watched as Kaddour gasped his final breath. The thugs fled, honor-bound to no one, particularly the dead.

Again, the falcon screamed overhead, triumphant.

Ala al-Din retrieved his miraculous hand and seated it back in place, striding with purpose back to the street, leaving the rubbish in the alley.

Someday, Shahin, he thought, *you and I will meet. But not this night.*

An Excerpt from

THE TOWN OF GROUND-DOWN GEARS

ELSPETH PENNYWORTH SCARCE REMEMBERED HER LIFE BEFORE SHEETS OF flame seared the night sky. She woke that fateful night alone, gasping for breath and crying out for her parents.

They never came. They never would.

At twelve years of age, she stumbled from her room to search the hazy hallways. The empty chambers. Her parents' room, with two still mounds beneath the blankets and the scents of copper and iron and burning saltpeter on the air. Whimpering, Elspeth backed away before turning to flee, stumbling down the stairs. She discovered Papa's workshop with all his things cast about as if his latest machination had exploded with industrious abandon, yet with no evidence of said artifact in sight. By the flickering orange glow lighting the far window, she rummaged around the room. Mostly by feel alone, she claimed what little she could of her father's legacy from beneath the debris. Everything from delicate watchmaker's tools to sturdier spanners to precious bits of invention only a fraction realized. They went into a makeshift satchel slung across her chest, created from Papa's scarred leather work apron.

By the time she had nearly all she could carry, acrid fumes robbed her of breath and fine soot caused her eyes to tear. Even so, she risked precious moments, scrambling to the flagstone hearth across the room. The custom fireplace filled the wall. It had served to heat the room and endless pots of tea, but also as both kiln and smelting box. Most importantly, however, as only she and Papa knew, it served as hiding place for his priceless journals.

Embers began to flutter down through the thickening smoke in a hellish parody of burning snow as Elspeth climbed into the firebox to pry up the flagstone in the far corner. Vapors creeping past the open flue filled the space, nearly overwhelming her as she grabbed her prize. Stumbling back to the door in a half-crouch, wracked with coughing, she flinched as the brass doorknob seared her hand. She nearly dropped everything. Tears coursed down her cheeks to salt the lip she caught between her teeth. She turned back to the room, her gaze going toward the far wall. Flames flickered brighter beyond the glass. She had no choice. Reluctantly picking her way across the room, she set down the journals and dragged a chair upright before the window. Elspeth climbed up and unlocked the avenue of her escape before pushing at the sash with all her might. As it shot open, she nearly fell through, wincing as she caught herself against the frame with her injured hand. Not even trying to hold back her sobs, she snatched up the journals and clambered through the opening.

Flames surrounded her. Hellish heat robbed her of her breath until she screamed soundlessly. Hunched over the leather-bound parchment containing her father's notes, she bolted over the clearest patch of ground, both her hair and the hem of her nightgown smoldering as blisters simultaneously rose and burst on her bare feet. She fled before billows of crimson-limned smoke and tongues of flame as the world burned around her, clutching Papa's journals in her arms as his prized tools thumped against her back. She had just enough sense remaining to drop them at the riverbank just outside of town before falling into the shallows.

It was a wonder she'd survived at all.

By the time she came back to her senses, the town of Trumbleton was no more. All she had known. All she had depended on in her young life. All she had cared for. Everything was gone, leaving behind charred remains and empty shells, with a handful of buildings on the outskirts only partly seared, but just as abandoned.

As Elspeth had been.

In the three years since that fateful night, no one had ever returned to rebuild. Nor even to investigate. Sure as hellfire, no one came search-ing for *her*. That wasn't to say there hadn't been scavengers trying to loot the things she needed to survive. Elspeth had learned how to scare them off well enough that some soul eventually painted over the town sign, changing Trumbleton to Troubleton. She found satisfaction in that. She wasn't ready to abandon her home, and she did not particularly care to have strangers claim any part of it for their own.

Setting those thoughts aside, Elspeth opened her eyes to the faint light of dawn creeping through her window. Almost since the morning her new life began, she had taken up residence in the mason's house. She had waited only for the flames to die away and the rubble to cool before exploring her options. This one had been chosen on the merit of it being built mostly of stone, thus mostly unscathed. Of her own home, nothing remained, save the grand fireplace from her father's workshop — very likely built by that self-same mason. Though solitary, her existence was not uncomfortable… now. As a young girl of twelve, even with the basic skills any frontier child already had — geared as those were to community living — it had taken her time to figure out how to survive.

Climbing from her bed, she stripped off her much-darned night-gown and examined herself in the oval mirror standing in the corner of the room, reminding herself she had survived. The dawn light was kind, softening the puckered ridges of the burn scar high on her right cheek. The one tugging the side of her mouth into a permanent smirk. Just the barest trace of burning pitch had slid off a rooftop as she fled the town, catching her across her face and the edge of her hair. She'd brushed it away with the hand already burned.

She thanked her stars every day that it had missed her eye.

Other than her right hand and the soles of her feet, both thick with scars, that was the worst damage her body had taken. As for the rest of her… while her hair had grown back, it was darker now, like tarnished gold, a little coarser and spiky. It never grew longer than the span of her hand, where before it had been silky and bright gold, falling down her back in a tumble of little-girl curls. Her body had likewise changed, grown into a woman's shape, with a woman's concerns, but thanks to an uncertain diet, remained lean, well-muscled, but balanced on the cusp between thin and too thin.

"Enough," she said aloud, her voice deep and throaty in a way it never was before the fire, but had been ever since. "There is work to be done."

The moment she spoke, a chirp sounded in the hallway. Elspeth twisted the lock and opened her door, grinning for true as a tiny calico catling saunter-stretched into the room, her tail curling in a lazy 's' over her back as she arched it and extended her opposite legs fore and aft with each stride. The little one came to sit at her feet, looking up at her with sleep-squinted eyes.

"Good morning, Ember," Elspeth murmured, meeting the feline's bright orange gaze. After a quick scritch, she turned away to dress. Long ago, she had scavenged the town herself, sorting through what little remained and claiming whatever might serve her in one manner or another. Over underthings that had come from the mayor's household, she pulled on a pair of young boy's tweed knickerbockers and a man's slightly too-large ghillie shirt, the laces dangling loose. Over that, she wore a thick leather vest she'd sewn herself, covered front and back with all manner and sizes of pockets, leaving her hands free when she foraged or scavenged, or her tools handy when she tinkered. She then pulled on thick soft socks to protect her feet before sliding them into work boots only slightly stuffed with butcher's paper found in the kitchen below. Lastly, she went down stairs, stopping to take her broad-brimmed plantation hat from its hook beside the mudroom door and place it on her head as she left the house. Her face and scalp remained sensitive to the sun. Together, she and the cat went to forage for breakfast.

Today, they needn't go far.

There on the flagstone before the door lay an odd jumble of edibles: two duck eggs, one hale and whole, the other with a webbing of fine cracks across its surface, but still intact; a snapped-off cane of brambleberries, mostly ripe; and a plump hare, the neck mangled beyond recognition, but the flesh and pelt otherwise unharmed.

Elspeth's teeth tugged on her lower lip from the inside as she stooped to gather up the offering. In her early days of solitude, she had comforted herself by making… companions. Crude, tinkered homunculi. Rough forms that echoed those people lost to her. It had only made things worse as she hadn't the means or the knowledge to give her friends even the illusion of life.

At first, anyway.

For those first months, she healed. For those that followed, she acquainted herself with survival and improving her situation. After that, she read. Cover to cover, she devoured her father's journals. And when she'd completed those, she scoured the ruins for any other books that might have survived. She'd found a few, not to mention all manner of other useful things she'd long since moved to her chosen residence.

Clothing and tools, preserved goods and bedding. Not a lot, and not completely unscathed. But more precious than all of that, at the ironmonger's place — another structure untouched by the fire, having been built on the outskirts to safeguard the town from… well, the threat of fire — she'd come across a precious order bundled and labeled and waiting to be collected, expressly meant for her father. Gears and struts, springs and coils of wire. Lubricant and bearings. Sheet metal waiting to be cut and shaped. Basic components her father hadn't bothered to manufacture himself. Among them, precious punch cards, thin strips of metal notched with holes in precise order. Punch cards meant to animate her father's inventions, each one designated for a desired task. Never tested. But she had read all about their intended application. Carefully she rewrapped the bundle and tucked it down her back, in the biggest of the pockets she'd cobbled on her vest.

It had taken a week, but she emptied that shop, claiming that forlorn order and everything usable besides, leaving in place only those metal-working tools that served no other purpose than the work that would be done in that place.

With the knowledge she had gained, and the components to stock her workshop Elspeth had set her tinkered toys upon a shelf and produced new automatons. Better, refined. Of new parts and useful function, thanks to her father's punch cards. More to give herself purpose and distraction in her idle hours, when the daily concerns of food and repairs and hygiene had been seen to.

Perhaps she would have reconsidered the wisdom of her efforts, had she known…

Author's Note: This was meant to be one of the stories in this book, but the tale has outgrown the intended format. I have placed this excerpt here as a promise to tell that tale, however long it might take. I hope you enjoy the beginning. And I fervently hope the rest is not long in coming.

About the Author

Award-winning author, editor, and publisher Danielle Ackley-McPhail has worked both sides of the publishing industry for longer than she cares to admit. In 2014 she joined forces with Mike McPhail and Greg Schauer to form eSpec Books.

Her published works include eight novels, *Yesterday's Dreams, Tomorrow's Memories, Today's Promise, The Halfling's Court, The Redcaps' Queen, Daire's Devils, The Play of Light,* and *Baba Ali and the Clockwork Djinn*, written with Day Al-Mohamed. She is also the author of the solo collections *Eternal Wanderings, A Legacy of Stars, Consigned to the Sea, Flash in the Can, Transcendence, The Kindly Ones, Dawns a New Day, The Fox's Fire, Between Darkness and Light*, and the non-fiction writers' guides *The Literary Handyman, More Tips from the Handyman,* and *LH: Build-A-Book Workshop*. She is the senior editor of the *Bad-Ass Faeries* anthology series, *Gaslight & Grimm, A Cast of Crows, Grease Monkeys, Grimm Machinations, Side of Good/Side of Evil, After Punk,* and *Footprints in the Stars*. Her short stories are included in numerous other anthologies and collections. She is a full member of the Science Fiction and Fantasy Writers Association.

In addition to her literary acclaim, she crafts and sells original costume horns under the moniker The Hornie Lady Custom Costume Horns, and homemade flavor-infused candied ginger under the brand of Ginger KICK! at literary conventions, on commission, and wholesale.

Danielle lives in New Jersey with husband and fellow writer, Mike McPhail and four extremely spoiled cats.

My Trusty Cogs and Gears

Andrew Hatchell
Andy Hsu
Brendan Lonehawk
Brooks Moses
Carl W Bishop
Carol Mammano
Carol Pafford
Chad Bowden
Christopher J. Burke
CJ Frost
Craig "Stevo" Stephenson
Dale A Russell
Deborah A. Flores
Ef Deal
Elaine Tindill-Rohr
Eron Wyngarde
Gary Phillips
GreenShirt52
Ian Harvey
J.R. Johnson
Jennifer L. Pierce
Jeremy Bottroff
Jerrie the filkferengi
Joanne B Burrows

Julian White
Kal Powell
Kelly Pierce
KJS Palmer
Krystal Bohannan
Kurt Beyerl
Lark Cunningham
Linda Pierce
Lisa Kruse
Lorraine J. Anderson
maileguy
Marie Devey
Phil Huffsmith
pjk
Richard Novak
Rob in AUS
Robert Claney
Scott Schaper
Steph Parker
Stephen Ballentine
Stephen W. Buchanan
The Belina Family
Tina M Noe Good
white beard geek